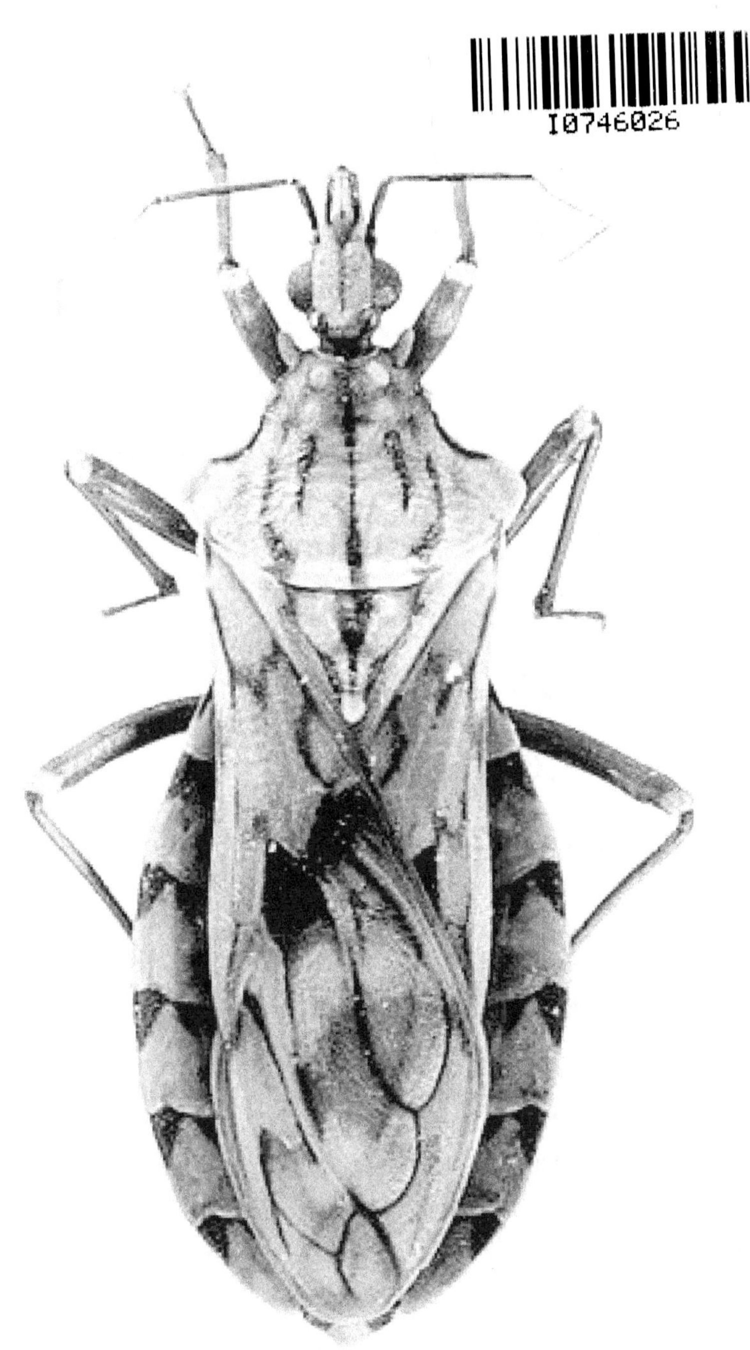
I0746026

Also by J.M. Holmes:

Retrievers (Anthology)

Ice, Ice, Baby (*with* Prodigy *and* Time Trial)

The Fruit-Eating Cat

Energy Spike

A Deep Breath of Water

Waking Up Outside

Little Potato Fries *(collected poems)*

Pro Tem: The Amazing Year (nonfiction)

All titles also available in large print and giant print editions

J.M. HOLMES

THEY LEFT ME FOR DEAD

LITERATI INTERNATIONAL

~ SINCE 1981 ~

Toronto • New York • London

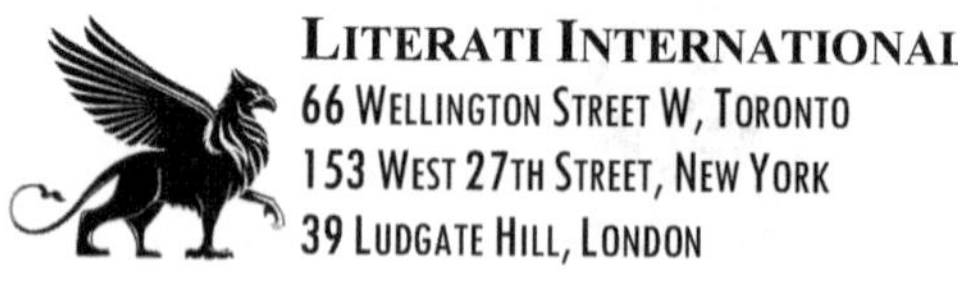

LITERATI INTERNATIONAL
66 WELLINGTON STREET W, TORONTO
153 WEST 27TH STREET, NEW YORK
39 LUDGATE HILL, LONDON

Library of Congress Control Number: 2021918766
ISBN 978-1-7368485-4-8

To Anne,
who always loved everything I wrote.

Rest in Peace, dear sister

Table of Contents

PROLOGUE

THEY LEAVE ME for dead, lying in a drainage ditch beside the road, and I can hear them as they drive away in my car, just a couple of good ol' boys lighting cigarettes and cracking jokes, as though they're coming back from a fishing trip and not from having just beaten someone to death.

I can't tell you how long I lie here, listening to the rain and the wind and the crickets and all the assorted night sounds that creep back to life after the humans have gone. The stentorian gasps of my own ragged breathing keep time with the persistent rustle of some weeds just off to my left, making me wonder if perhaps some hungry wild creature is assessing my potential as a snack. I am slipping into and out of consciousness every few minutes, and in a grey recess of my mind I peripherally hope that I will be insensate when the beast finally decides to start gnawing on whichever part of my body it's going to eat first.

Every so often a vehicle shoots by in the night, faintly announcing itself first with the quiet hiss of its approach, then gradually crescendoing into a deafening rattling roar defining its identity as car, pickup truck, or 18-wheeler. The weeds around my head sway and buck convulsively as the vehicle whizzes past my location, and then in the wake of its passage quickly resume their motionless witness to my suffering.

I have no way to alert the passing drivers to my presence. I can't seem to move my arms and legs, or even turn my head, either because some part of my spine is damaged or merely just because the intense pain from the rest of my body is overwhelming all my other senses. I know that several of my ribs are broken, along with at least two of the fingers on my left hand. My sides throb in excruciating pain, and I assume that I am bleeding internally from several damaged organs. I can't really see at all from either of my eyes, as both are swollen shut and caked in blood. The taste of blood fills my mouth and I can't breathe through my nose.

I lie here, face down in the dirt and muck, and I wait – for death, or the dawn. I have no way of knowing which will arrive first.

PART I

endless SUMMER

*"If I owned Texas and Hell,
I would rent out Texas and live in Hell."*

– General Philip Henry Sheridan

welcome to my world

THE WEEK had started like any other summertime week in rural west Texas — hot dry wind in the morning announcing the beginning of another 16 hours of suffocating heat.

The afternoon's punishing gales that fling sand and grit into eyes squinted almost shut against the merciless blazing sun are just a value-added bonus.

Normally I enjoy the mornings, at least until about 8 am. Before the day catches on in full force it's actually kind of pleasant, what with the few remaining birds flitting through the post-dawn sky and the majority of humanity still ensconced in their homes.

Recently, though, a troublesome wave of immigrants from Central America has swept into our county, disturbing the peace and harassing anyone who ventures outdoors. The scientists refer to them as *"Reduviidae"* but most of us just call them Assassin Bugs.

They showed up in our county much as many other visitors do, with little fanfare and with no one really taking much notice. They're nothing new, of course. Some even consider them a welcome sight, as their primary food source is other insects, especially the aphids, caterpillars, grasshoppers and sawflies that attack the cotton plants, our county's main source of income.

But we've never seen them before in such abundance. And this particular variety is different from the rest. Bigger. More aggressive. While the kind we're used to usually don't bother us much, these new arrivals quickly distinguished themselves with random assaults on unsuspecting humans.

You can be leaning up against a fence post in a field, maybe casually chatting on the phone with your Aunt Maybell, when out of nowhere an assassin bug will make a beeline straight at you and impale you with its spear-like mouthparts, injecting a blast of excruciatingly painful toxin that sends you staggering and gasping for air. It's no mystery why one of their other common names is Ambush Bugs.

The attacks aren't so frequent that people hide indoors or anything like that, but any sighting of a swarm will quickly empty a local park or playground, and the farm workers have all taken to wearing more generous clothing and wrapping hand towels around their necks, where the bugs seem to like biting the most.

From time to time you can see a swarm of them rocketing past, but more often they'll appear individually, sometimes fleeing when you come upon them in your garden or out in the field, exploding up out of the foliage like a surprised cat and whizzing away into the ether before your eyes even have the chance to focus. Other times, though, and this is the behaviour that hasn't won them any friends among the good residents of our fair county, they come straight at you out of nowhere, small bloodthirsty kamikaze vampires hurtling full-throttle at any unprotected area of your body.

They seem to be especially active at night and very early in the day, and the constant threat of being assaulted turned my morning stroll into a nervous trot, forcing me to stay cautiously alert listening for the tell-tale hum of an approaching bug – a hum that quickly escalates into a loud buzz right before the tiny beast makes contact.

I'm not scared of them but I'm a sensible man, all the same. I don't stick spoons into whirring blenders or try to beat the train across the tracks, either. Trouble usually finds those who take unnecessary risks.

But it's time for breakfast and I'm damned if I'll let a few bugs keep me from bacon and eggs, not to mention a good cup of coffee. Everyone has their Achilles heel and mine is a pronounced inability to make proper coffee. Years of trying and failing have convinced me that it's one of those tasks best left to the professionals, like doing your taxes or adjusting the timing chain on your car. I've long-since waved the white flag on the coffee battle, and so every morning you can find me heading downstairs from my flat above the pharmacy on Main Street and hoofing it over to the only café in town open at 6 am – hell, the only café in town, period. We do have one other eating establishment, but it's more bar than restaurant, notwithstanding its optimistic appellation as *"Bud's Country Dining"*, and the few meals they serve-up in the afternoons and evenings look like they've come straight out of TV dinner packages and dumped onto the plates.

But the *Early Riser Café* is worthy of its name, opening up at 5am for all the worn-out farmers, ranchers and truckers looking for a hearty helping of fuel to carry them through the first part of their day. The food is good and the servings are generous, and word has gotten round, so that there are often at least a dozen tables occupied by 5:30am. Not bad for a town of only about 900 souls.

We were a vibrant community once long ago, a thriving collection of farming and ranching homesteads, sitting on a jog in a two-lane road between Pecos and the New Mexico border. Before the interstates were built we used to get a lot of tourist traffic stopping in for gas or eats on their way to or from Carlsbad Caverns, but all that has long since dried up along with the well water, and these days our little strip of highway sees more jackrabbits and coyotes than cars.

The café isn't a long walk away from me, only three short city blocks, just over half the total length of what only an unbridled optimist would refer to as our town's "commercial district". The pharmacy underneath my flat sits smack-dab in the middle of this short grey strip of dead or dying businesses that constitutes our downtown area. Across from me, on the south side of the street pressed up against the funeral parlour on the left, is the bank. Slate-grey slabs of polished granite on a solid, squat building that's easily over a hundred years old.

The designers tried futilely to mitigate its intimidating appearance by incorporating a large picture window into its façade, and during banking hours a person on the street can see on the other side of the glass silent shapes with serious faces moving around conducting serious business, but when they close up for the day someone comes to the window and does something with a cord that lowers big wide venetian blinds until the window becomes just another featureless space on a big featureless wall.

To the right of the bank is our town's only Accountant. The Accountant's office doesn't have any big picture windows but the people who pass in and out look just as serious, nonetheless. The remaining still-operating businesses on my particular block are mostly one- or two-person operations – a hardware store with poorly-lit aisles crowded with overloaded shelves holding items that look like they've been there since World War I, a hair and nail salon, and a boot repair shop where the same set of boots have been on display in the window since the day I moved here, and for probably long before that. Their presence on the streets is punctuated with the dark, unoccupied spaces of former businesses that eventually succumbed to the general malaise typical of all dead-end towns in other dead-end areas of the country.

Near the end of the second block on my route is the storefront of a combination real estate/travel agency. The window to the left of the door has about a dozen photos taped along it just below eye level, displaying the various farms, houses, and mobile home lots currently available for purchase. Some of the photos have been up since I arrived in town, but every so often there's another one or two added to the list, and a little more rarely, one or two of the other photos disappear. Whether the properties have been sold or the owners finally just gave up hope is an open question.

On the window to the right of the door is a large colour poster of a beach with the requisite leaning palm tree and empty chaise longue reclining in the shade. I suppose the implication is that it's waiting for your butt to come validate its lonely presence, but to me it just seems sad, a constant reminder of days lost forever, opportunities missed, trips never taken and plans delayed until it's too late. I wonder how many people have passed by that poster and thought, 'Yeah, one day I'm going on that trip,' thinking that thought every day, only to finally discover that their next trip was one-way, six feet underground. And the chaise stays empty.

But every day just before I pass by and see that poster, I hope that maybe today there's a beautiful blonde in a tiny bikini sitting there now, sipping away on a Piña Colada and giving us a sexy come-hither smile, letting us know it's not too late and if we hurry up and book that flight, we might be in time to join her before she finishes that drink. But so far, she hasn't shown up. And the chaise stays empty.

The wind exhales a sudden burst and little dust clouds billow up momentarily from the sidewalks that line both sides of the streets, then settle back down into invisible little thin blankets on the cement. The sidewalks don't get much use here. Just about the only time you see someone walking in our community they're carrying a gas can.

I'm the local exception, possibly because I'm not a native here but a recent transplant from places that are much busier, where people move around in a hurry rushing to finish their day so they can wake up early and get a head start on their next day of rushing around. There's nowhere to rush to here, and not much to do when you get there, which suits me just fine, and I take my time walking to the *Early Riser*. When the bugs aren't hunting me, that is.

The café sits off by itself, just past the west end of the downtown strip where the row of tight-packed businesses ends and the lots widen out to include little parking areas. On the northwest corner to my right is a farm implements store occupying what was probably about a century ago a very majestic two-storey house where Someone Very Important once lived. But now the main floor has been opened up, the claustrophobic interior walls removed, fluorescent lighting installed and a large portion of the front wall replaced with glass. What was probably once a perfectly-manicured lawn is now a gravel parking lot, where a large sandwich-board sign advises passers-by that a variety of animal feed can also be found on the premises. The parking area is empty except for a single rusted pickup truck carefully parked at the far left side of the row of spaces. Inside, a lone figure is moving around working in low light, moving between the back area and a cashier's station.

On the other side of the street opposite the feed store, sitting on the southwest corner with its own set of parking spaces, is a white one-storey concrete building. The top half of the front wall is all glass, a long window running the length of the building, where evenly-spaced pillars and little sets of red-and-white checkered baby curtains tied up into hourglass shapes break up the expanse of window into little five-foot-wide units. A large, carefully painted sign mounted on the roof identifies the place as the *Early Riser Café*. The sign looks like it's been there a while, but the letters are still very readable so Management hasn't yet felt the need to prioritize its renovation over other more-pressing tasks. It's almost 5:45 am, so the parking area is already full and behind the length of glass several pairs of faces facing each other in profile fill the spaces between the red-and-white checkered curtains.

I can't imagine what could inspire someone to operate a restaurant in a one-horse town in the middle of some of the most barren landscape in America, and the café's current owner, Renault, is offering no clues to answer the riddle.

A friendly, unassuming man somewhere in his 50's, Renault speaks excellent English, but smothers his syllables in a thick French accent that imbues his establishment with an exotic air that most people around here have never encountered before in their entire lives. He's small and wiry, as though God had experimented with making a human out of pipe cleaners, and he's filled with a seemingly inexhaustible store of energy, always in movement, bustling between the tables and the kitchen, carrying dishes, greeting customers, working the cash register – the living embodiment of the phrase "chief cook and bottle washer".

Renault has no relatives in Texas, or anywhere else in the US, for that matter. He likes to tell the story that he came to Texas because he figured he would find kindred souls in Paris, TX, but that when he went there the first thing he saw was a 65-foot replica Eiffel Tower topped with a cowboy hat. The sight was so disconcerting he left town and drove west as far as he could until his car broke down in our humble little burg.

I'm pretty sure the story is apocryphal, but like the other people in town I honour his decision to keep his true motivations private. People around here don't like to pry.

In fact, no one actually even knows Renault's real name.

"Renault" – pronounced "ren-no" – is a nickname he's been given in honour of his defunct automobile, a Renault 4, one of those ugly French 4-cylinder cars that filled the streets of every town in France in the 60's.

Renault told me once that back in France he'd had a Citroën 2C, a famously-reliable car better known as the "Deux Chevaux" – or "two horses", in honour of its two-cylinder engine – and he'd wanted to buy one just like it when he arrived in America. But the only French car he could find for sale was this Renault, so he'd coughed up the cash and managed to make it as far as our lovely slice of heaven before some essential part beneath the hood gave up the ghost. Owing to the decided lack of Renault mechanics and foreign automobile parts stores in our bustling metropolis, our newfound arrival ended up becoming a permanent resident. At least, that's how Renault tells it.

He took a job as cook at the *Early Riser* but it wasn't more than two or three months later that the owner decided early retirement was preferable to slowly frittering away his remaining life savings on a dying café with steadily dwindling receipts. Renault somehow came up with the cash to buy the café and it was then that the eatery began its marvellous evolution.

He immediately set about transforming the café into a little slice of French heaven. He bought new curtains and bright red checkered tablecloths and filled the walls with framed reproductions of famous artworks that he bought from the art school in Odessa. Expensive, custom-made banquettes were shipped in from a furniture place in Atlanta, and huge new walk-in refrigerators and a gigantic new grill were installed in the kitchen. He added whimsy to the menu, with such entries as "Pablo Picasso Scrambled Eggs" and

"Van Gogh Roasted Ear of Corn". He pipes-in French songs and serves the coffee in wide bowl-like cups. He stopped short of running a channel from the river Seine through the middle of the café, but I'm sure he considered it.

At first, our startled residents didn't know what to make of the restaurant's metamorphosis, but quite quickly the bill of fare made converts of them all. The food is delicious and abundant and, combined with Renault's indefatigable good humour, invariably turns any occasional diner into a regular. Truckers even detour to stop at the *Early Riser* and farmers change their schedule so they can begin the day with one of Renault's delicious creations.

There are only two employees at the *Early Riser*: the cook, Manuel, whom Renault hired the day he bought the place; and Jenny, a local girl in her late 20's, a pretty blonde farm girl whose husband stepped out one night to replenish his beer supply and then skidded off the road and right into a tree after hitting an armadillo taking an evening stroll on the highway. At her husband's funeral she had shared with Renault the uniquely-Texas knowledge that armadillos will jump straight up in the air when startled, and often impact with cars' undercarriages, causing wrecks far more often than one might expect.

The young lady's quiet equanimity in the face of devastating loss had impressed and moved Renault, and he'd offered her a job on the spot, which she immediately accepted.

I wouldn't go so far as to say that that is when events began to unravel, but it certainly stands out as a moment that ended up impacting pretty significantly on the lives of Jenny and Renault, and eventually, on mine as well.

JENNY

I **HAD ALREADY** been eating at the *Early Riser* for months, of course, but before I met Jenny I was merely a customer, showing up for breakfast and lingering over coffee and conversation with a few regulars. Renault is friendly, but somehow I'd never gone past the *"how ya doin'?"* phase of our relationship.

It would have stayed that way, except one afternoon shortly after she signed on at the *Early Riser*, Jenny showed up in my office looking for help.

The front part of my flat above the pharmacy is set up as an office, although it's really less an office than a big unused space acting as a buffer between my living quarters and the door. Its prime features are a big desk and chair and leather couch left over from the country lawyer who used to occupy the space. I use it now as a place to store dust.

In an unbridled fit of ambition one day I replaced the handwritten sign I'd taped on my door with a proper one that reads, "Master Tradesman". It was the best description I could come up with. I am known locally as a jack-of-all-trades, with knowledge I've picked up in a dozen different countries spread out around the globe. My dad worked for the State Department and dragged his family along with him wherever he was posted. I never quite cared for school, but that doesn't mean I was averse to learning – I just got my education on the streets, instead of in classrooms.

I spent time in India hanging out with an electrician who could fix anything that plugged in. I palled around in Hong Kong with an engineer who kept the famous Peak Tram working, and in Switzerland I learned to ski from a former Olympian. I still keep in touch with acquaintances in Africa, South America, and Eastern Europe, and when I need to I can ask their advice on matters as wide-ranging as medicinal herbs, microprocessor technology, or international finance.

But now I live here, in the ass-end of Texas, soaking up the peace and quiet and picking up a modest income working whatever jobs fall into my lap.

I landed here almost by accident, sent to repair a farmer's faulty GPS unit on a harvester. I woke up the next morning to find a dozen notes slipped under my motel room door from other farmers needing help with their technology-laden machines. In the course of taking care of those jobs, word got out that I can also help with tax problems via my friendship with a fellow I'd known in Zurich who now works for the IRS. After that, thanks to a casual conversation about holistic remedies that I'd had with a worried mother of a rashy preschooler, calls started coming in seeking advice on dealing with allergic reactions to local flora and requesting help in dealing with a variety of invasive species of bugs.

I traded my motel room for a cheap flat above the pharmacy on Main Street, scrawled my name on a piece of paper and taped it over the lawyer's sign on my door, and have spent the last three years learning to love life in slow motion.

And when I open my door and see Jenny standing there, biting her lower lip like she's trying to teach it a lesson and twisting her car keys between her two clenched hands, I know this is going to involve a lot more than fixing a recalcitrant tractor or finding a lost dog.

She's a pretty young thing, too pretty for this small town, but still too young to know it. By time she wises up she will have lost the advantage and become just another sagging middle-aged woman wishing her life's path had swept her as far away from this dead-end town as Greyhound could take her. But today she's still a fresh, shining package of possibilities, and, as she stands there looking up at me from beneath eyelashes that spread like miniature bicycle wheel spokes above two big pale blue eyes, I find myself wanting to be the knight in shining armour that she is obviously in need of right now.

"I'm sorry," she says.

"Sorry for what?" I ask, genuinely curious what this girl

could possibly have done to me which would require an apology.

"Oh – well, I wouldn't normally drop in on someone without calling first for an appointment, but I had no phone number for you and didn't know how else to reach out. I didn't want to bother you at the diner. I'm sorry if I'm disturbing you by showing up unannounced."

Despite the girl's obvious state of distress, I can't help but smile at this last remark.

"Hmmm. Well, I see the problem. I'm not sure if I can help you right now, though. After all, it wouldn't be fair to all the other people who've been waiting hours to see me." The door is open wide enough that she can see past me into my office; it looks just as deserted and unused as one of those roped-off rooms you see in preservations of famous people's homes — *"And on the left, you can see where he composed his magnum opus, working at that very desk,"* and the tourists take pictures and then shuffle on to the next room containing more musty-smelling antique furniture. I could easily have understood if she'd taken a camera out of her purse and snapped a picture before asking what was next on the tour.

But instead, she looks terribly disappointed and almost starts to turn around and leave until she suddenly looks up into my eyes and says, "Oh. Yes. Very funny. You're making fun of me."

"No, no I'm not," I say quickly. "I'm just trying to lighten the mood. You look worried. I didn't want you to feel uncomfortable. Please, come in." And I step back to allow her to enter.

She eases hesitantly into the dark room and as I flip the light switch I notice her imperceptibly pausing before she moves to sit down on the dust-covered chair in front of my desk. Her clothing is modest, but clean and attractive. She's wearing a short-sleeved pink blouse, buttoned up just high enough to be socially acceptable in mixed company but still far enough open at the top to remind men what's important in life. A small gold cross on a thin gold chain glimmers in the low light against her creamy skin beneath her perfect neck, nestling into the little valley of her cleavage. Her tight, sky-blue pencil skirt is mid-thigh length and her sensible shoes have the perfect amount of heel to give her calves a pleasant curve. She has a sense of style, but it is obviously subservient to a restrictive budget. I contemplate what a striking figure she would make if she had the financial resources to dress in garments other than those found at the local women's clothing store.

I move around to sit behind the desk and as I settle in I watch her carefully, trying to figure her out. I've seen her a few times at the café already, but I haven't really gotten to know her. I know of her husband's recent death and that she lives on a small ranch just south of town, but that's the extent of it.

She has shimmering blonde hair that she kept tied in a tight bun during the times I saw her working at the café, but right now it's hanging loose and cascading down over her shoulders in a gleaming mane. Her makeup is discreet and well-done. There are no two-inch strips of eye shadow or thick lines of mascara, just a slight blush on her cheeks. Her dark pink lipstick stops well before the corners of her mouth, giving her a pixie mouth, not quite puckered but offering a hint of what that might look like. Her eyebrows are soft, thin lines with slight, delicate arches. Right now they're pulled together in a worried frown.

She's still nervously biting her lower lip and in the thirty seconds it takes me to get settled and to move aside some dust-covered papers laying on my desk, she crosses and uncrosses her legs three times. If her perfectly-painted white French Tips weren't so nicely manicured, she would probably be chewing them down to their nubs.

I don't mind her crossing and uncrossing her legs. She could go on all day doing that and it'd be just fine by me. She has nice legs, and lots of them. They're long and smooth and slightly tanned, not leather-brown but not sickly pale white either. She's not showing them off on purpose, but her skirt rides up nicely when she sits down, which makes her pull the hem toward her knees with her hands, and every time she recrosses her legs she has to do it again. It means she has to stop twisting the car keys around for a second, but after every time she tugs her skirt she goes right back to torturing them.

"Here," I say, pulling a bottle of Scotch and two glasses from the lower drawer in my desk, "You need a drink."

"Oh, I could never –" she begins, but I cut her off.

"Oh yes you could," I reply. "You're wound so tight right now your fingers could squeeze diamonds out of a lump of coal. This is purely medicinal, as far as I'm concerned. If you don't relax a bit we might as well just call this whole thing off right now. I need my clients to think clearly if they're going to give me all the information I need to do a good job."

She looks hesitant for a second more, then reaches out and picks up the glass I've put in front of her on the desk. She lifts it to her lips and in one gulp swallows the whole drink. She doesn't put the glass back on my desk, but keeps gripping it in her right hand. The keys are getting a much-needed breather but I'm concerned the glass might shatter from the strain.

Eventually a bit more colour fills her cheeks and her panicked eyes settle into a more relaxed gaze. She releases her eyebrows and the glass at the same time, placing the tumbler carefully on the edge of the desk and removing her hand very slowly, as though she's afraid it might slide off of its own volition and she'll have to reach out and grab it midair before it hits the ground. With her eyebrows back where they belong she finally stops looking like a cornered animal.

"Well," I say. "That didn't take much convincing. I didn't think you'd drain it in one swallow, though. That's 12-year-old Scotch. You're supposed to savour it slowly."

"Are you still trying to lighten the mood, or have you switched to making fun of me now?"

I laugh out loud.

"There you go! See, you're relaxing already," I say between chuckles. "Maybe now you can take a deep breath and tell me why you've come to see me."

*   *   *

It's an old story, a familiar story, one repeated probably hundreds of thousands of times throughout the course of human history.

In the wake of her husband's death, the cockroaches had crawled out of their holes to come pick at the remains.

Within one week of the funeral Jenny had been visited by no fewer than three different scumbags seeking to snatch up the prize left unprotected at the family farm. Said prize being Jenny herself, of course.

"I suppose it's partly my fault," she says, characteristic of the typical victim's sense of culpability. "I told them at the funeral how much I appreciated their good wishes. I just never thought they'd take that as an invitation to move in with me.

"They caught me off-guard, at first, but as soon as I realised what they were after I told each of them I need time to mourn, and that I want only to be alone. Two of them were quite nice about it, really. They wished me well, and promised to reach out again in a few months. It's the third one that's become a problem."

She pauses to pick up her glass again, which I have refilled, and this time she sips at the amber liquid a bit more pensively.

"He was Marty's 'partner', I guess you could say. Marty never confided in me what exactly he was doing to earn money, he said it was rebuilding cars but there was too much cash coming in for that to be true. I should have known better but you know how it is when the money's good and life is easy – the hard questions never get asked, do they?"

I don't answer. She's on a roll now and I don't want to distract her.

"I'm thinking it was Meth. Marty would come home with some kind of God-awful stink on him, and he worked the strangest hours. People who rebuild cars don't work at night, normally, I'm pretty sure."

She stops to sip at her drink again. I'm not sure she even realises I'm still there – she's speaking more like she's talking to herself in the dead of night after a catastrophe, going over events in her mind, audibly sorting out the details.

"And this guy, this Willie, he was always coming around and ogling me, making dirty comments, and Marty never said shit to him, just told me to go in the back or to go to town when Willie came by. Then they'd head off together to God knows where in that piece of shit truck he died in, and I wouldn't see Marty again for a day and a half. But he always treated me well and he certainly wasn't stingy, so I kept my mouth shut and my fingers crossed."

Another swallow, and I refill her glass again.

"And now that Marty's gone Willie is pretty upset. I don't think he can do whatever they were up to without Marty's help, and he says he deserves some kind of split from their 'company profits'.

"If that was all it was, I could deal with that. Marty left a lot of money locked up in a trust fund of some kind, administered by some firm over in Houston, and I can't touch it until it matures or something. I've got the paperwork and I showed it to Willie and he didn't understand it any better than I do but it's pretty clear that no one is getting their hands on it for several years, and even then not all of it at once. I guess Marty was a lot smarter than I gave him credit for.

"And a lot of the spending money Marty gave me I used to pay for my mother's retirement home in El Paso – she's got Alzheimer's and needs round-the-clock care. Luckily, I paid up front for the whole year just a couple of months ago. But I don't think mom will last out the year, so I'm not too stressed out about that bill, at least.

"But with Marty gone and the money all locked up I'm reduced to working for tips just to keep the lights on. Thank God the farm is paid off. Something else Marty did right, before he went and wrapped himself around a tree.

"But now Willie isn't talking about the money anymore. He thinks he's got some kind of right to *me*, now, too. He came round every day last week and got worse every time and pushier and pushier and last night it got real bad and he grabbed me hard and pushed me down and if I hadn't pulled a gun on him you can guess how that would have ended up."

She stops talking for a moment and pulls up her sleeve to show me a huge purple bruise on her upper arm just below her shoulder.

"He's not done with me, I know that. He'll be back the next time he's got a belly full of liquor, which shouldn't be too long from now, and he won't let me pull a gun on him twice."

I feel the time has arrived to ask a question. Telling the story has sent her back into a nervous wreck, notwithstanding the alcohol she's consumed, and I want to slow her down.

"What about the Sheriff? Would he be of any help at all?"

"The Sheriff is Willie's cousin," she says flatly. "You do the math."

She doesn't say any more and I wait about half a minute while her breathing slows back down to normal. When we've both used up all the amusement value in silently staring at each other I exhale deeply and sit up a bit higher in my chair.

"I'm not sure why you think I can help you," I say. "First, I abhor physical violence of any kind. I've always regarded violence as the last refuge of the incompetent, and short of killing this fellow I'm not sure what kind of action would keep him from coming back. These kinds of guys don't just wave a white flag and move on, you know."

"I never said I wanted you to kill him," Jenny says softly. "I don't know what I want you to do, and I didn't know what to expect when I knocked on your door. But word around town is that you can *do* things, can find solutions that other people can't. I need a solution. I need *something*."

We sit there again in silence for another moment, each of us contemplating the situation from our own unique perspective. A rattling hum fills the room, spilling out of the window-mounted air conditioning unit on the street-side wall. The box blows out a gentle stream of super-chilled air, sending dust motes spinning through a crack of sunlight that bleeds through a slender gap in the closed window blinds. My chair creaks slightly as I shift my weight, and I look up into Jenny's eyes, two eyes that cling to me as their only hope in a merciless situation.

"OK," I say. "I'll help you."

Her relief is tangible. Her shoulders noticeably relax as the tension that had been gripping her body suddenly dissipates in the wake of my announcement.

"But I can't do anything until tomorrow, at the earliest, and it's not safe for you to go back to your farm, not until I've dealt with Willie. Does anyone know you've come here to see me today?"

"No. I wasn't even sure myself I should come. And there's no one I can confide in. I'm really alone."

"Not anymore you're not. You've got me. Now give me your phone and your car keys – I assume you're parked on the street out front. What does your car look like?"

I leave her alone in my office while I drive her car across town to a junkyard garage belonging to a friend of mine called Jorge. He was running a crew of farm workers when I first met him, but he's branched out now to auto salvage, and his cousin handles the crew while Jorge wheels and deals auto parts and sells them on the internet. There are over two hundred car corpses in his lot, surrounded by a high fence.

People used to drive long distances to pick up the parts Jorge pulls from the deceased autos on his lot, but once his nephew set up a website for him his business doubled and the in-person traffic all but disappeared. It's the perfect place to stash Jenny's car while she lays low.

Jorge comes out to meet me as soon as I show up at the gate. He's wiping grease off his hands with a clean white rag and smiling broadly as he walks out. We are very good friends and he greets me as though I'm a close relative he hasn't seen in years.

JORGE

I **HAVE BEEN** living here only a few months when I first meet Jorge.

He's a quiet man, hardworking, serious, carrying the weight of responsibility on his shoulders from managing a crew of two dozen farm labourers while also taking care of his own extended family. A wife, four children, two sisters and their families, along with the grandmother and grandfather and a variety of cousins, all of them living in a sprawling ramshackle ranch house sitting on a couple of acres of desert.

There's no reason why our paths should ever cross, but one particularly warm morning I'm returning from breakfast when I open the street door to the stairs leading up to my office and Jorge is standing inside, at the foot of the stairs, gripping a tattered wide-brimmed floppy hat with both hands as though it's a shield protecting his groin.

He's dressed in clean blue jeans that are just beginning to fray at the bottom, a pale work shirt and heavy, well-worn work boots. There's a small embroidered logo on the breast pocket of the shirt, but it's for a big agricultural company headquartered in Amarillo, so either he got it as a giveaway promotional item or bought it used at the local thrift store. His hair is neatly trimmed but obviously a home job. He's clean shaven and his fingernails are short with the faintest dark line beneath the end of the nails. He has all the indications of being a man who cares about his appearance but doesn't throw away his money on it, either.

"Um, hello," he says, in unaccented English. "I have a small problem and I hear you help people out sometimes."

"Let's talk upstairs," I say.

My door still has the handwritten sign taped on it that I put there the day I moved in, and I notice for the first time how creased and worn out it's looking, and I make a mental note to put up a proper sign when I have the time. We move inside and sit down in the outer room. I offer him a drink from the bottle I keep in my desk drawer but he shakes his head. I'm about to pour myself one when I think better of it and suggest maybe he'd prefer to join me in a cold beer.
He pauses for only the briefest moment before he smiles and says, "Yes, I think a beer would be perfect. It's a hot one out there today."

"It's hot every day. Where do you think you are, anyways? Don't you own a map?"

That brings a laugh out of him and we crack open our beers and I settle back while he starts right in on his story.

"My name is Jorge Delgado, and I have a crew that works at the McAllen farm."

I let him go on, but he could stop talking right there – I can guess at his problem without too much effort.

The McAllen spread has a reputation in our town. It's notable mostly for the presence of its owner, a bitter Texan with a chip on his shoulder, a flat-out loser named Dusty who'd married into money. Dusty had been stepping-out with the only daughter of a local cotton farmer when the old man had suddenly paid the price for a life spent eating steaks and bacon. Dusty was sharp enough to know to strike when the iron is hot and almost before the Will had been read he'd knocked-up the newly-minted heiress and talked her into a quickie wedding in Reno.

He'd never worked so hard at anything in his life, and it was the last time he ever would work, as from the day of their wedding he's never again held down a job or pulled his weight, preferring to leech off his new wife's money and to drive around his wife's farm bossing around the workers.

He has no apparent life skills, aside from a prodigious appetite for beer, and is a loud, rude drunk, but a typical coward, never picking a fight with anyone his own size. Naturally, he's universally reviled in our community and is regarded alternately as a laughingstock or an arrogant pain in the ass. A long time ago during one of our country's brief periods of peacetime he had been in the Service for about five minutes and now he never lets anyone forget it, always the first to stand up and be recognised at Veterans' Day events, and always sure to ask for his veteran's discount on any product or service he purchases. He's lathered his truck in bumper stickers advertising his past military association, and is almost always wearing a t-shirt proclaiming his affiliation with the nation's fighting forces.

His wife has long-since seen his true colours and has lost all respect for him, which only adds fuel to Dusty's fire. To make up for his wife's emasculation he throws around his weight wherever he can.

I take a long swallow and listen to Jorge's story. Sure enough, Dusty figures prominently in it.

"One day my crew and I were taking our break when Dusty came across us. He didn't seem to think we should be resting and, well, you know how it is, words were exchanged and tempers flared, and before long he was threatening to call the Border Patrol on me and my crew and have everyone thrown out of the country.

"I'm legal, you know. I was born here, but some of my crew are… ah, without papers. I backed down when he started making threats, and we all went back to work, but Dusty didn't let up.

"He told us we wouldn't be getting paid for that week's work because he'd caught us 'goldbricking', as he put it, and he said he figured we owed him for pay we'd gotten without doing a full week's work. He said we should count ourselves lucky we still had jobs.

"If that had been the end of it I could put up with it, but he's been returning almost every day to harass me and my crew. He's been riding us mercilessly, berating us and yelling at us to work harder."

"It makes sense," I say, "He got a real sugar high when he got you to back down the first time. Now he's hooked on the feeling. Once you feed a coyote he keeps coming back for more."

"We can't go on this way. One of these days one of my crew is going to haul off and plow that loudmouthed asshole, and that'll be the end of it for all of us. The first thing Dusty will do when his jaw heals up enough for him to talk again is call the Border Patrol. I can't let it go that far. We need to stop it now."

"I can't promise you anything," I say, but as soon as the words leave my mouth Jorge's face lights up. "There's no reason to expect that I can have any influence over Dusty. But I'm willing to try."

Jorge is already standing up, and he reaches down into his pants pocket and pulls out a wad of squashed bills.

"No, no," I say. "Nothing 'till the job's done, and even then only if I can find a way to help you."

"No." he says firmly. "Win or lose, I pay my way. No one works for free. Take my money or you'll hurt my feelings."

He smiles as he says this and I return the smile, reach out and take his money.

dusty

HE NEXT MORNING I start following Dusty. He drives to Odessa twice every week to pick up supplies or to do other business, which I find suspicious in the extreme. Not only does he have no apparent responsibilities or duties at his wife's farm, there surely isn't any reason he needs to drive a few hundred miles every week not to do them.

I don't have to work hard to find out his secret. He's so confident in his own cleverness it never occurs to him that someone might be watching him.

When he gets to Odessa he drives right through town directly to a quiet residential district where he parks his pickup truck against the curb in front of a tidy little house. It's a pleasant little one-storey bungalow, white trim with blue shutters, with two large hydrangea bushes standing guard on either side of the front door in a modest lawn of perfectly-trimmed pale green grass. A cow-shaped mailbox is mounted on a post beside a narrow cement walkway that leads directly to the front door tucked beneath a tiny wooden awning, also painted blue and white. From where I sit about three houses away, parked in a slip of shade under a huge Cathedral Oak, I can just make out the shape of a little wooden artwork on the front door in the form of a bluebird sitting in a nest surrounded by little eggs.

Showing better fiscal judgment than the civic planners of my own town, the city of Odessa has not bothered to pour sidewalks along these streets – the lawns come right up to the curb. I look up the street past the house, then I turn around and look down the street behind me. There are about twenty houses within my range of vision, and if there's more than five different floor plans I'd be surprised. It's a planned community of starter homes for middle-class suburbanites, and to their credit most of them look like they are trying really hard to make the best of it. The lawns are trimmed and healthy, the yards are neat and the street is clean. The American Dream, if not writ large, then writ honestly.

Dusty gets out of his truck and ignores the little cement walkway and strides across the perfectly trimmed lawn then between the hydrangea bushes up to the door and, using a key, enters without knocking.

For the next three hours very little happens. Every so often, about once every half hour, a car or a service truck of some kind quietly glides down the street, passing the silent sleeping houses. I have a bit of excitement for a moment when I see a cat strolling along the top of a fence by a house to my left, but for the most part even the flies are showing the good sense to stay inside out of the heat. I don't want to call attention to myself any more than I can avoid, so I keep the engine off. Which means no air conditioning for me, thank you very much. All the windows in my car are down but that helps only when there's a breeze of some kind to move through the vehicle. The air outside is so still I could blow a soap bubble and it would drop as straight as a pebble. I'm starting to miss the midafternoon abuse I usually suffer from the dry wind that constantly sweeps through my town. But this sleepy little neighbourhood is so quiet and well-behaved even the wind is afraid to barge in and start throwing its weight around. The buzz of a lone cicada bleeds down from a tree a few houses distant, and I'm impressed by the courage the bug shows in interrupting the quiet. Eventually he gets the message and shuts up, though, and the eerie silence descends once again on the block.

Finally, the front door of the house opens and Dusty emerges, stomps across the grass to his truck, ignoring the little sidewalk again, and drives away.

I don't bother following him back home but keep watching the house. I figure I can tolerate about one more hour before I literally melt and the city will have to come sop up my liquid corpse off the front seat of my car. But my patience is rewarded about forty-five minutes later, when the garage door on the little house starts rolling up and a minivan emerges and backs down the driveway. I can just make out sitting in the driver's seat an attractive young brunette talking on her phone and not looking in my direction at all. She drives to the local Piggly Wiggly and I gladly follow her in, shuddering with pleasure as the air conditioning envelopes me. With great difficulty I restrain myself from jumping onto the open bin of frozen fish and rolling around in the ice chips, and instead pretend to browse the shelves while the woman works her way through the store picking up supplies, which seem to consist of mostly chips and beer and ice.

She looks to be a Mexican-American hybrid, somewhere in her very early thirties. Her complexion is the perfect degree of healthy creamy-tan Mexican pigmentation that evokes just enough of her Aztec heritage to imbue her with a sensuous, exotic flavour. Big brown eyes and long dark lashes surmount classically high cheekbones and perfect, full red lips that occasionally part to reveal two straight rows of gleaming white teeth. Her breasts are generous and high on her chest and in perfect proportion to her body, which looks to be fit and toned, with a small, tight derriere and long, smooth legs.

She's wearing a short, flattering blue-and-white sleeveless dress that's both slender and elegant, and attractive blue open-toed shoes with two-inch heels and little white straps that wrap around her ankles. She could be mounted on a post in the front yard of her house and be perfectly in sync with the colour scheme. Her ears are pierced with tasteful little gold studs and her long fingernails and neatly-trimmed toenails are all painted the same deep red colour as her lipstick. What little makeup she's wearing is invisible but you know it's there, applied so expertly you can barely tell. Her hair looks smooth and shiny, like the shelf of water at the top of a waterfall just as it starts over the edge. It shimmers the same way, too, and sways gently around her neck and shoulders. She looks as out of place shopping in the Piggly Wiggly as a Ferrari at a tractor pull. I'm pretty sure she would look out of place just about anywhere in Odessa.

When she moves to the checkout I make sure to get in line behind her, standing close enough to smell the aroma of jasmine and honeysuckle, and I wonder whether it's coming from her shampoo or perfume. When she pays for her selections she pulls the bills from a generous wad of cash bulging in her pocketbook. I don't bother following her out of the store. I've seen all I need to.

On the drive back home I contemplate all the possible interpretations of what I witnessed. The rhythmic thrum-thrump of my tires passing over the seams in the blacktop imparts a meditative beat to my thoughts, keeping time to the white lines disappearing beneath the corner of my car's hood, their silent stroboscope providing a visual accompaniment to the tires' metronomic tics. I squint through the heat shimmering off the asphalt stretching out before me, an endless straight scar splitting the moonscape of barren quasi-desert and stunted trees that spread out to either side as far as the eye can see. By time I get home I've come to a lot of different conclusions based on a lot of hazy assumptions. I need to narrow down my choices.

I warm up a frozen dinner in the microwave and try to summon the strength to eat it. Sitting in a car for four hours in 100° heat is more draining than one might expect, and after struggling through dinner I sit in my office in the dark, sipping at a glass of warm Scotch and listening to the rattling air conditioner waging its never-ending battle with the heat outside, until I climb into bed and pass into unconsciousness.

I keep my eye on Dusty for the next few days. Based on what I've noticed in the past, I've figured out that on the days when he intends to visit Odessa he first stops in at the *Early Riser* around noon and gets a coffee and a sandwich to eat on the drive. This gives me the opportunity I've been looking for to verify my suspicions.

The next time Dusty stops in for his road-trip snack I'm already sitting eating lunch at the long counter that runs between the open kitchen and the tables along the front windows. I've chosen the seat closest to the register, just to my left, and have a large coffee in a to-go cup that I've been letting cool down to room temperature. There's a tight plastic lid on the to-go cup, with a little mouth hole at its edge.

Dusty walks in like he owns the place and thinks we should all fall down and genuflect when he enters. Renault comes over to the register and looks at him expectantly, drying off his hands on a small clean hand towel tucked under the half apron wrapped around his waist. When Dusty places his order he speaks as though he's addressing a particularly stupid child, overstressing and overenunciating each syllable, breaking the words into little pieces that escape from his lips bit by bit. When Renault disappears into the kitchen Dusty stays standing in the same spot blocking the register, imperiously glowering at the room. Probably wondering why no one is genuflecting.

When he gets his order he reaches down into his jeans, pulls out a thick sheaf of bills and peels off a ten-spot that he thrusts out at Renault. As he stuffs the fat roll of bills back down into his pants pocket, I raise up on my stool a bit and lean forward, stretching out my right hand to pull some napkins from a countertop dispenser. When Dusty picks his coffee and sandwich up off the counter I tilt my coffee cup in my left hand over his bulging pocket, hiding my action by craning forward even more, and direct a generous stream of lukewarm coffee straight down into his pocket, where it immediately soaks into the folded wad of bills. I'm ready to make loud apologies, but he doesn't even notice what has happened.

He takes his sandwich and coffee and heads out the door and I watch him from my place at the counter as he guns his truck engine, throwing up a handful of gravel as he spins the vehicle around and bounces out onto the road. There is no indication that he's discovered yet that he has a pocket full of sopping wet bills, and hopefully when he does he'll just figure he spilled his own coffee on himself without realizing it, and be too lazy to care much.

I'm chuckling to myself thinking I've just pulled off the smoothest move ever, when I notice I'm not the only one chuckling. The booth nearest the café door is occupied by a single grizzled old rancher, a fellow I know by acquaintance, but not so well you could call us friends. He obviously witnessed "Operation Coffee Spill" in its entirety, and every indication is that he finds it the funniest thing he's likely to see all day. His chest is bobbing up and down as he laughs quietly, emitting soft half-wheezing, half-grunting noises that sound like a Model T Ford struggling up a steep hill, and little tears are showing in the corners of his eyes. Like I said, there's not a lot of love lost between Dusty and the other residents of this town. He probably thinks I did it as a prank, and his eyes are sparkling as he grins widely at me. I raise my finger to my lips in the universal hush gesture, and he responds with a knowing wink. I'm pretty sure he won't be blabbing about my little maneuver, but as I walk over to the door he raises a hand and holds it out like a little stop sign. I softly smack my palm against his and can still hear his asthmatic wheezing giggle as I open the door and step out into the bright sunlight.

I'm in no hurry to get to Odessa. There's not much attraction in the prospect of sitting in a hot car watching grass grow, but I've got something I need to do in the city, so I settle in and start on down the road.

Once I get to Odessa I head downtown and look up on my phone the location for the main office of Odessa's Utility District. It's a squat white building on the edge of the business district that sits shimmering in the heat like a mirage, the air in front of it rippling like an ethereal harem dancer. The windows are dark, coated against the merciless sun, and give away no hints about the interior of the building. They could be conducting human sacrifices in there behind the opaque black glass windows, and no one passing by would be any the wiser. I park in a diagonal spot in front of the building and walk up to the entrance, where I pull on one of the tall vertical chrome handles running down the sides of two large dark glass doors, and enter into an ice-cold oasis of linoleum and fluorescent lighting. There's a long counter in front of me with five service windows built into it, but there's a person behind only one of them. No human sacrifices are currently in progress.

I walk up to the service window and make noises about opening an account. The person behind the counter sends me off to the side where there's a row of small offices, where I sit down with some tired looking man in a tired looking suit sitting behind a desk in an office utterly devoid of personality or warmth. The sole personal touch is a small little stand on the desk holding the fellow's business cards. "Cletus Moore, Customer Service" is embossed in tiny blue letters beneath a large imprint of the Utility District's logo and address. I discreetly pluck a few cards from the little stand while the man peers at his computer screen. There's a small rack of brochures standing on the floor beside the desk, with titles like, *"Energy Conservation and You"* and *"Water: Our Most Precious Resource"*. I wonder what high-school Communications class created these startling bundles of insight. I grab a couple of each brochure and tuck them into my suit jacket's inner breast pocket.

Mr. Moore has just assembled the appropriate forms for me to start filling out when I make a sudden exclamation and tell him I've forgotten something important, and rush out. He sits at his desk and watches me leave and looks down sadly at the papers he has just printed off for me. There's no place in the barren little office for blank paperwork and I wonder how long it will be before the forms make their way to the recycling bin, or if maybe he'll perform a minor act of rebellion and tuck them away in a drawer to use on the next customer.

I leisurely drive down the street wondering how much more time I should give Dusty to complete his visit when I spot a cobalt blue neon sign glowing on a door in an otherwise featureless white stucco wall that connects seamlessly with the front walls of a half-dozen other businesses along Main Street. The sign reads *Arctic Zone Icehouse* and that's all the encouragement I need to nose my car into a diagonal parking spot butting up against the sidewalk. I leave the windows down and don't bother locking the car as I walk away. Anyone who would be compelled to boost my car in the middle of the afternoon in 100° heat needs it far more than I do.

The bar is predictably dark and quiet. It's not quite cold enough for me to see my breath in the air. A dozen or so customers who look like they might be regulars sit in small clumps in a couple of booths, or side by side along the bar.

The bartender barely looks over as I walk up and settle down onto a stool at the bar. He's an absolute giant, eight feet tall if he's an inch, and the patrons sitting on the other side of the bar from him look like children in comparison. When he gets to my end of the bar he towers over me and I'm momentarily puzzled. Close up, I notice his body is all the wrong shape for his height, as he looks neither tall and thin nor big and wide. I lean forward a bit and squint down at the floor behind the bar — it's raised a couple of feet above the floor of the rest of the room. The bartender watches me patiently. I'm obviously not the first person to notice the setup.

"The owner's a dwarf," he says, heading off the inevitable question, leaning forward and down to bring his face within a few feet of mine.

"I think they want to be called 'little people' now."

"Naw, I think just the midgets want that. Dwarf is fine."

"I'll take your word for it. Let me have a glass of whatever you've got on tap."

"We've got three. No preference?"

"Yeah. It should be cold."

He straightens up and moves away without asking anything else and a moment later reappears in front of me with a glass filled with amber fluid. It's exactly what I asked for.

In the next forty-five minutes I drink three of them, slowly, watching the bartender moving around his domain quietly tending to business, a human watchtower looming over the rest of the room, occasionally bending down to serve the patrons seated at the bar. The job must be hell on his back, and I wonder what the turnover rate is for his position. Looks like a Worker's Compensation claim in the making.

At one point he comes out from the behind the bar to go retrieve some empty glasses abandoned by a table's former occupants, and he suddenly loses his dominant aura, becoming just another regular-sized human performing a mundane task. Somehow it's disconcerting to me. I had come to regard him as a colossus striding through the bar ready to smite miscreants and to perform whatever superhuman feats might be called for. Now he just looks feeble in comparison to his former persona. I can't help but feel a bit saddened by the change.

I toss enough bills on the bar to cover my drinks and a respectable tip, and I move toward the door. He's back behind the bar and headed over to pick up my money but I still can't see him again in his larger-than-life image. Now he's just a normal guy on stilts, and the illusion has been spoiled for me forever. *Sic transit gloria mundi*, I suppose.

Fifteen minutes later my car glides into the same spot three houses down from Dusty's truck, also parked in the identical place as before. Nothing at all looks any different from the last time I was here. I think it might be a few degrees warmer, but nonetheless the air feels the same, the sun and the heat feel the same, even the rebellious cicada pipes up once and briefly launches the same futile buzz from his tree. I sit there just as I did before, and hope without success to spot the cat again.

It's my lucky day, though. About an hour sooner than I expected, Dusty leaves the house, strides across the lawn, climbs into his truck and roars away. Within thirty seconds of his departure the entire street is once again a still life painting, and I'm left sitting in my car soaking my shirt with perspiration.

AN HOUR LATER I'm still sitting there and I've come to the conclusion that the lady inside the house isn't running any errands today. Time to take the bull by the horns.

I pull out from my spot and drive to the end of the block, turn the corner, and park out of sight of the house. I get out and reach into the back seat of my car, where a clipboard is laying. There's about a dozen sheets of paper on it clamped on top with a metal claw. I printed up a bunch of meaningless squares and lines of text on the top one last night. As long as no one tries to actually read it everything will be just fine.

I pull the brochures from the Utility District office out of my suit jacket that's laying on the front passenger seat, stick them underneath the claw on the clipboard, and head on foot back down the street. I'm dressed in a short-sleeve white shirt, a loosely-knotted thin black tie, plain black slacks and black Oxfords. I leave the suit jacket in the car.

Unlike Dusty, I stick to the little cement walkway as I approach the house's front door. The wooden artwork with the bluebird and eggs is more than just decorative, I notice. The center of it features a little brass knocker jutting out from the wood that sends a sharp *tak! tak! tak!* through the door and into the house as I pull it back and tap it against a matching tiny brass plate.

There's no peephole or glass in the door, so the person inside has to open it to see who's calling. A lady pulls it back about six inches and peers at me from behind the crack. What little I can see doesn't look very welcoming. She inspects me with one suspicious eye that she lines up with the crack and says, "Jess?"

"Good afternoon, ma'am," I say as I poke Cletus Moore's business card at her through the crack. "I'm here from the Utility District and we're just going house to house letting people know about our water conservation programs and taking a quick survey."

"Not interested," she says, and the door starts to close.

"We're paying people for their participation," I say just before the door clicks shut. I have to pull my hand back quickly before the door shuts on the business card I'm holding out.

The door opens again immediately. The same six inches, but there's more interest now in both the eye and the voice, which says, "How much?"

I can see her eyeballing my clipboard and the brochures, which I hold in plain sight. I move the business card back into the crack and this time a set of fingers appears and pulls it out of my grasp.

"Fifty dollars per survey, in cash, and it's only three questions. Takes about a minute."

"Fifty dollars to answer three questions? Paid in cash? Nothing else?"

"Nope. Nothing to buy, we're not selling anything. Just want to know your opinion."

Before she can think it over I reach into my pocket and extract a few hundred-dollar bills, and I start flipping through them so she can see.

The door opens wider now and it's the same woman I saw the last time I was here.

The blue-and-white dress and tasteful shoes have been replaced with a white silk robe that comes down just far enough to block my view of the Promised Land, and is loosely tied with a matching silk cord. The generous breasts I admired earlier appear even more abundant now as they press against her robe, pushing the two sides far enough apart to create a revealing gap that extends almost to the cord around her waist. She's barefoot now but that doesn't make her legs look any less appealing. Her hair is just-showered damp and hanging limply but somehow even more sensuously around her face, which is not harmed at all by the lack of makeup. The air around us is filled with the fragrance of jasmine and honeysuckle, which settles the perfume-or-shampoo question.

I stop riffling through my money long enough to pull a couple brochures off the clipboard and hand them to her, then I make an annoyed sound and look up at her apologetically.

"Oh darn, I'm sorry, all I have are hundreds. I guess I've already used all my fifties."

I make as though I'm going to turn around and she immediately says, "That's OK. I have change. Hold on. Don't go away."

She's in such a hurry to go get her money she doesn't even bother closing the door, and leaves me standing there looking into her tidy little house while she disappears to get her purse. The room I can see is immaculate, with a clean, neat little loveseat sofa in the center with a clean, bare end-table at each end, a potted plant on the floor in the corner, and a couple of tasteful nondescript paintings of tasteful nondescript landscapes on the two walls I can see. It doesn't look like anyone has ever spent any time in the room. Even the potted plant looks lonely. Within seconds she's back at the door with her purse, and she opens it and I see sitting in it a thick wad of bills. Immediately I smell the reek of coffee.

"I'm sorry, my husband spilled coffee all over his money this morning, this one is still a little damp, do you mind?" and she pulls a fifty from her purse and holds it out toward me tentatively.

"Of course not," I say, and hand her the hundred then accept the fifty she's holding out to me.

"I'm glad you had cash," I say. "So many people these days never keep much on hand. It's all cheques and credit cards."

"Oh, no, we're not like that. My husband insists on paying for everything in cash, we never write cheques."

"Well, that's certainly one way to protect yourself from identity theft, anyways. If you don't leave a paper trail everywhere you go, you're much safer."

"Let me see," I say, looking down at my clipboard, "Um, have you heard about our new time-of-day water meters?"

"Is that one of the three questions?" Her eyes are twinkling. Ever since she saw the sheaf of centuries in my mitt her attitude has become tangibly more friendly.

"Um, well yes, actually. It is. We need to know if our message is getting out to the public."

"Well, I don't really pay much attention to that," she says quietly, looking directly into my eyes without blinking. "My husband takes care of all the bills. He pays them in person down at the utility office. I never even see them. I have a little home… salon. You know – hair, and nails, and… massage…."

"We don't have you listed as a commercial property," I say, studiously flipping through my make-believe paperwork.

"Oh! Well, it's sort of informal, if you understand. This neighbourhood isn't listed for businesses. I mostly work on… friends. Very low scale. Are you going to have to report that?

She's switched from looking coquettish to worried. I give her what I hope will pass for a reassuring smile and say, "Oh, it's not my job to report that sort of thing. I guess it can be our little secret." And I wink conspiratorially at her.

Her face brightens again and she says, "Oh, thank you! What's the next question?"

Before I can reply she cuts me off and says, "Oh, how rude of me, making you stand outside in this awful heat – why don't we sit down inside for the rest of your survey?"

And as she says this she discreetly adjusts her robe, swapping the order the sides are crossed over each other, and in the process giving me the briefest microsecond of a flash of her naked body. It's almost subliminal, it's so quick, but the image of her perfect breasts and creamy tan skin sears into my retinas all the same.

I'm momentarily frozen, and she looks into my eyes again and smiles, the tip of her tongue barely showing as she slightly wets her lips. It clears up in my mind exactly what kind of services her "salon" specializes in.

I decide the time has come to make a quick exit and I say, "Oh, well, considering this isn't really your home, I guess we can skip the next two questions. You can keep the fifty, though. I appreciate your time."

She looks disappointed and says, "Oh, that's too bad, and I was just starting to enjoy our conversation. You look like such a nice person. I meet so few nice people. You're sure you need to go right away?"

A big part of me really wants to stay. I can't think of a better way to spend the next couple of hours than to let her entertain me in her salon, but I recall with a shudder that Dusty has just been here, and all that separates him and me is a quick shower. I smile at her and shake my head.

She takes it well, although I'm sure the image of my sheaf of hundred-dollar bills is still hovering in her mind's eye. Knowing that she and I have different visuals throbbing in our brains helps me to put a brave face on it, and I thank her again, turn around and walk back down that neat, no-nonsense little cement walkway up to the cow mailbox, step over the curb and turn right, and stroll back up the street.

Before I reach the corner I turn and glance back at the little blue and white house, and I see she's still standing in the doorway watching me, as though to let me know it's not too late to change my mind and come back for some afternoon delight. I guess business is a little slow here in the burbs.

On the drive back home I call Jorge and tell him I have what he needs. We arrange to meet tomorrow.

In the morning Jorge is waiting for me again when I come back from breakfast, standing in the same place in the same pose as the first time I met him. This time, however, he doesn't look concerned. He looks hopeful.

We head on up the stairs and he can hardly contain himself behind me. It's as though I'm leading a puppy. I get us a couple of beers and we settle into our respective chairs as we pop the cans open and each take a long swallow.

"You can have this," I say as I lean forward in my chair and stretch my arm out over my desk to hand him the coffee-soaked fifty.

He looks at the bill quizzically and I say, "I got that from the woman Dusty is paying to have sex with twice a week in Odessa."

Jorge's eyes get so big in his head I'm afraid he'll pop his optic nerve. His jaw drops open and he audibly gulps.

"It gets better," I say quickly, throwing a one-two punch of information at him just for the fun of it. "He's also paying the bills for the place where they're making the beast with two backs, and I'm pretty sure she 'entertains' other clients in the place, too."

"That doesn't just make him a cheater, it also makes him a sucker," I continue. "And if his wife finds out how much of her money he's been paying this woman, she won't be satisfied just cutting off his dick and balls, she'll want to see him starve to death in the streets, too, kid or no kid. The only thing that pisses off a woman more than her husband stepping out on her is him spending her money to do it. If Mrs. McAllen finds out about this, it will be the end of Dusty."

Jorge has recovered enough from his initial shock to finally say something, and he asks, "So you want me to give this to Mrs. McAllen?"

"No, I don't think that would be a good idea, my friend. The messenger of bad news never gets away quite scot-free. If you give that to Mrs. Dusty and tell her the whole story she'll feel humiliated, and there'll be blowback. She wouldn't be able to bear seeing you in the fields after that – she'd think you and your whole crew were laughing at her, and eventually you'd get the boot. No, there's a better way."

"What would that be?"

"Well, it's a dirty word, and one I would never normally use, but a scumbag like Dusty sort of falls outside the normal bounds of decent behaviour. The word I'm thinking of is 'blackmail'.

"You give that bill to Dusty and he'll immediately know who you got it from. You won't have to be very explicit for him to realise that his entire life now depends on you keeping your mouth shut. I might go so far as to say that now your two roles are reversed. You call the shots and Dusty has no choice but to play ball or to say goodbye to Easy Street.

"Don't abuse your new power too much, though. Slimeballs like Dusty can take only so much before they lash out. If I were you I'd quickly negotiate a new 'employment contract' with Dusty, making sure he understands that his best interests are intimately connected with his ability to stay out of your way. Once he can't harass you and your crew anymore he'll find another target, but that should provide you with a lasting peace. Out of sight, out of mind, as the saying goes."

"I – I don't know how to thank you…."

"All part of the job, Jorge. You paid me for my time. As far as I'm concerned we're square."

"No, I don't think so," he says, taking my hand and pumping it furiously. "We're a long way from square. I won't forget what you've done for me. And whatever I can ever do for you, if you don't ask me to do it, well… you'll hurt my feelings." And he gives me that huge smile of his.

I laugh out loud and we clink our cans together.

RED

E HIDE Jenny's car at the end of a row of crumpled Toyotas, then Jorge gives me a lift back to my flat so I won't have to hoof it through the stifling heat.

In the middle of the day the combined effects of the economic downturn and the midafternoon heat render our burg a virtual ghost town. We drive through deserted streets past boarded-up storefronts and dark shop windows. The stores that haven't closed permanently are shuttered until late afternoon. Residents here take their mid-day siesta seriously, as the intense heat all but turns the asphalt into soup. The electronic sign on the farm implements store flashes "109" at us as we drive by. I assume that means 109 in the shade. I wonder how hot it is in the middle of the street. Fried-egg territory, no doubt.

A tremendous *thwack!* barks at us from the windshield and both of us jump in our seats, and then we break into laughter to see that an especially large assassin bug has flown directly into the glass and pulverized itself into a green and black oozing splotch. Jorge turns on the windshield wipers and sprays a stream of fluid at the corpse, and after several passes most of it is wiped away.

"Well, that's one fewer of those mothers to ambush us," he says, chuckling.

"Amen to that, brother," I reply, although I'm pretty sure that the lack of any one of the beasts won't make much of a dent in the local population.

I make him detour to the Piggly Wiggly so I can pick up some supplies, and treat him to a six-pack of his favourite brew to thank him for his trouble. When I get back to my flat I find Jenny laying on my couch snoozing peacefully. I wonder how long it has been since she has taken a nap without wondering who was going to wake her up by knocking at her door.

She looks good laying there. It's a sight I could get used to. I'm not interested in tossing my hat into the ring with all the other cockroaches, though, so I dismiss the idea from my mind. Girls like Jenny inspire all the right thoughts in men's minds, and all the wrong ones, too.

She gets up when she hears me moving around in the kitchen, and we put a couple of frozen dinners in the microwave and eat a quiet meal without saying much. I feel bad that I can't take care of her problem until tomorrow, but I have a prior obligation tonight and if everything goes well, it might be of help in my efforts to dislodge Willie. Jenny uses my phone to call and leave a message for Renault, referring vaguely to a "family matter" and telling him she'll call him when she's able to return to work. Until the Willie matter is settled I don't want her setting foot outside this apartment. I can't help but feel that that's a pretty strong disincentive for me to work quickly, though.

We watch a game show on the TV and then come across "Die Hard" playing on one of the vintage channels. I am momentarily depressed to realise that it now qualifies as a "vintage" selection – wondering what that says about me, who as a child saw it in the theatre when it first came out.

After the movie I go into my office and lie down and take a nap, then around 10:00 I change into a pair of dark pants and a black t-shirt. When I come back out Jenny and I argue over who's taking the couch and who gets the bed. I lose, and agree to let her sleep on my couch. I show her where to find clean linens and give her a pair of my sweatpants and a large t-shirt for pajamas. I tell her I'll be back late, so she should lock the door and not go out. Since the only phone I own is in my pocket, I leave knowing she is safely and anonymously tucked away safe from harm, at least for tonight, anyway.

For tonight's job it's crucial that no one see or recognise me. I keep checking my rear-view mirror as I head west on the road out of town, and after about thirty miles turn south into the night. There's no moon out and the darkness is absolute. My aging headlights dimly illuminate the one-lane road I've turned onto. It's paved, but only barely, and there's no center line to navigate by, forcing me to peer carefully through the narrow tunnel of light lest I accidentally lose track of the pavement and sink a wheel into the dusty clay shoulder. When I drove this route during the daytime a couple of weeks ago I'd felt tiny and insignificant as I passed the looming towers of oil derricks rising on all sides from the scrub-covered land. I still feel tiny and insignificant heading deeper and deeper into the vast stygian darkness, but that's Mother Nature's fault now and not an illusion created by some steel monstrosity designed by human engineers. At a bend in the road my headlights briefly shine onto a derrick rising up before me, and then sweep off to the side as I follow the curve, and the tower is swallowed up once again by the night. In the brief instant it was illuminated, though, it didn't seem to be especially huge or intimidating but rather just an ugly spire of dirty metal festering on the earth like a huge blister needing to be lanced, and I realise that the immensity of the endless night has robbed the construction of its power, much like a formerly-gigantic human bartender stepping down from a raised platform in a dwarf-friendly bar.

I'm on my way to the back end of an enormous ranch owned by a local man in his early 50's who goes by the name of Red. If he has a last name I've never heard anyone use it, and it doesn't seem as if he's needed it in the last few decades. Everyone knows who you mean when you refer to "Red". He and I often meet over breakfasts at the *Early Riser* and are on friendly terms, mostly just shooting the breeze on mornings when neither of us has any pressing duties to take care of. Which in my case is pretty-much every day.

I think back to my visit to his villa a couple of weeks ago, standing in his office, gazing at the endless acres of scrub through a picture window not quite as large as the jumbotron at Yankee Stadium. Wondering what the first settlers thought when they arrived in these lands, and why they'd thought it worthwhile to fight a war just to steal the land from Mexico.

At first, when I pulled up at the main entrance to his property that day, I had thought for a moment that maybe I'd taken a wrong turn somewhere and had accidentally stumbled into one of those desert spas that very rich people retreat to when they're caught in a sex or drugs scandal.

The house, if you can call it that, is the size of a small hotel, and the entranceway alone is large enough to drive through. White stucco walls surmounted by wide, shallow roofs covered in curved ceramic roof tiles stretch away on either side of a long passageway leading into an interior courtyard, widening out in places to accommodate the occasional decorative fountain or group of potted cactus plants. Various sets of wrought iron double French doors built into the walls betray the presence of large rooms on either side.

There was no one in sight when I arrived, so I left my car by the entrance gate and headed to the courtyard and the villa's front door about fifty feet in front of me, advertising its presence in the form of a pair of huge oak doors with long ornate brass strap hinges that extend almost completely across them. The doors look as though they could withstand a siege, and I wondered briefly if Red knows the Mexican-American War is over.

Grasping ahold of a hubcap-sized horseshoe hanging against a brass plate on the right-hand door, I pull it up and let it fall back against the gigantic door three times, marveling at the echoes that fade away into the depths of the house.

The first normal-sized thing I see since arriving is the little Mexican maid who bustles up to the door in response to my knock, and ushers me into a large, cool atrium.

"Meester Red, he out riding," she tells me with a huge welcoming smile. "He feexing a well. He say let you een when you come and geeve you sommteen to dreenk."

I decline the drink but let her lead me through the sprawling villa, passing a sunken living area that opens out onto a massive stone-covered outdoor patio with a built-in firepit the size of a large hot tub. After passing several other rooms we finally come to Red's office, and she leaves me there to wait for his arrival.

Everything in this house is Texas-sixed. Red's office isn't quite big enough to park a jumbo jet in, and it's the smallest room I've seen in the house. The burnt sienna tile floor is covered in Mesoamerican rugs, not just one big one but several of them, some crossing over others, disappearing underneath huge overstuffed leather couches and hulking coffee tables. At the far end of the room an empty fireplace the size of a garage door sits brooding silently behind a life-sized tarnished bronze statue of a cowboy riding a horse that's bucking up into the air on its hind legs. The horse looks like it's having a great time, and the cowboy on his back couldn't be happier. Just looking at it makes me want to be a cowboy, too, so I can have some of that fun they're enjoying.

The walls are lined with bookshelves, but instead of books they're filled with Native American artwork – baskets, pottery, paintings, wood and leather creations, little statues and large masks, feathered head-dresses, suncatchers and ornaments of every imaginable kind.

My inspection is interrupted when Red walks into the room, all boots and spurs and ten-gallon hat and cigar. The kind of man who acts like it's still 1848 and it's his manifest destiny to conquer and subdue the hardscrabble that stretches out of sight past the horizon. Looking out at the oil derricks that infect his land like a disease, I can't help but feel that the land is about as conquered and subdued as it will ever get.

He's full of Texas swagger but comes by it honestly. He's big and broad-shouldered, stands six feet and several inches, has a Texas-sized belly that bulges out above his belt, and hands like small hams. He's wearing his usual wide-brimmed caramel-coloured Stetson hat, clean blue jeans and a blue denim shirt with a tasteful plaid pattern. The bolo tie around his collar has little silver tips on the ends; there are also silver caps over the toes of his cowboy boots, and a matching silver belt buckle that is just barely visible beneath his stomach. A thin coating of dusty clay on his boots betrays his morning's activities, but other than that he is the perfect picture of the gentleman rancher.

He sees me looking at his artworks and says, "The wife's responsible for all that. Can't get enough of the shit. Not me. I think most of it's garbage. All that mystical mumbo-jumbo about the sun and moon and wind. No wonder we took the country away from them without even breaking a sweat. Hell, they were too busy dancing and singing to their buffalo gods to fight back properly."

I can't think of an appropriate response, at least not one that won't get me punched in the mouth, so I don't say anything.

"I hope you didn't have any trouble finding the place," he says, standing at his office bar pouring healthy portions of Scotch into two highball glasses. "Your phone's GPS probably crapped out on you halfway here – the cell service sucks in this area."

"I was fine. You gave me good directions."

"Well, I've had plenty of practice. The difficulty in getting here has always been one of this ranch's best features. If I wanted an endless stream of visitors I'd live in town."

He hands me one of the two glasses he's poured then settles into a big brown leather office chair that's behind his desk. Grunting with effort, he bends down and unclips and yanks the spurs off his boots.

"Good Lord," he says, leaning back, "My dogs are barkin'. I'm getting' too old for this shit."

I take a seat in a comfortable overstuffed green leather armchair on my side of the desk. The chair is big and solid, with little brass rivets running down the edges on both sides, as though it wants you to know it can take whatever load you park in it. I lean back and let the chair surround me, but unlike Red I resist the urge to stretch out my legs and to put my boots up on the desk.

"Problem is, though," continues Red, looking down at his drink and talking into it as though I'm inside his glass, "When you're this far off the grid and have this much land to keep an eye on, it can attract the wrong element, if you know what I mean."

I'm not sure I do, so I keep my mouth shut and wait for him to enlighten me.

"I might never have discovered the bastard, if it hadn't been for the flash flood we had last month. You remember the rain storm?"

"Hard not to. It was the only thing anyone talked about for the following week."

"I hear you, brother. Fifteen minutes it lasted. Don't sound like much but you know what happens to that rain when it falls out here?"

It's a rhetorical question, I suppose, because Red doesn't even pause.

"The ground's baked so solid the water just sits on top of it and don't sink in for shit. And if there's so much as a five-degree tilt to the land, all that water just cascades like a god-damned waterfall, gathering steam until it can knock over trees or whatever else is in its way. I've seen ten-foot walls of water come from even small summer storms.

"Got a little arroyo on the ass end of my land, it's usually bone dry but when the rain hits, it becomes a raging river for about twenty minutes. And in that twenty minutes it can unearth the most god-awful things. Which can include bodies.

"Human corpses, you get me? Some of the wetbacks the coyotes smuggle over the Rio Grande, if they haven't been sold into slavery and haven't paid extra to be smuggled farther north, are just abandoned as soon as they cross I-10. And they head overland in this direction. Right through my land. And sometimes die here. No water, 110° heat, that's all she wrote, brother. And when we get a flash flood it sweeps the bodies into the arroyo."

"And you go out and retrieve them?"

"Have to. It's my Christian duty, brother. No man should have human bodies rotting unburied on his land."

Red lifts his hat up only just far enough to wipe his forehead with a handkerchief, then lowers it back down onto his head. I've never seen him without his hat. He probably bathes wearing it. I wonder if he takes it off when he goes to bed.

"And when I went out riding last month after the storm, there weren't any bodies but I found something worse."

"Worse than dead bodies? Please don't tell me you're talking about zombies."

Red leans his head back and lets loose a thunderous belly laugh. It's the loudest I've heard him laugh since I've known him.

"Zombies I could deal with! No, what I found actually scares me, and that's not something I admit to very often."

That's probably true. I'm surprised to hear him admit it even now.

"Meth. It's the curse of this county. Sucks the life out of anyone who starts using it. But what you really got to watch out for are the Meth *labs*. Little huts tucked away in the middle of nowhere, stink to high heaven, dangerous as all get-out. Can blow sky high in a blast you can see and hear for miles."

"That what you found? A Meth lab? What did you do? Call the Sheriff?"

"Good God, no! You think I want a target on my back? I have a family to take care of. It gets out that I'm responsible for shutting down a lab and the Mexican cartel that owns it will make an example of me and my family. You don't poke the bear, my friend."

"I thought Texans aren't afraid of anything."

"Don't let anyone sell you that line of bullshit. Any rancher who denies that he's scared as shit of those Mexican crazies is lying through his teeth. Or crazy himself. Those people don't operate by the same set of rules as the rest of us. Hell, they don't have any rules at all, far as I can tell."

"I take it this is why you've called me."

"Well, I'm not stupid enough to stick my nose in their business, but I can't have a drug operation on my land, neither. Shit happens. Next you know, there'll be a turf war or some other problem and my family's picture will end up in the newspaper above the caption, 'innocent bystanders'. So far you're the only person I've told about this."

"So you want me to get rid of the Meth lab without involving you, or spilling the beans to anyone else, and I have to do it in a way that there's no blowback in your direction."

"Haw! I knew you'd get the picture! Son, if you can do this I'd be mighty obliged."

"Is there any reason for you and your family to leave town for a few days, a vacation, maybe?"

"As it just so happens, my niece is getting married in two weeks in Houston. The wife and kids are anxious as hell to get off the ranch for a few days. I hate to travel, but I could handle some time away from this place."

"That's when I'll do it, then. When you're out of town. It's the best deniability you can get."

"Haw! That's mighty white of you, brother. Mighty white indeed."

And now, two weeks later, here I am in the dead of night heading off to poke a bear. In its eye.

THE METH-HEAD

**HERE'S A SMALL** dirt path, really just two ruts in the dirt, that branches off an oilfield service road on the backside of Red's land, and it's obviously this track that the Meth dealer uses to access his lab. I drive about 100 meters past the turnoff and pull off the service road and tuck my car behind a Mesquite tree that's somehow found a way to survive in this moonscape. I pop the trunk and pull out my night vision goggles, along with a pair of work gloves,

a baseball bat and a full-head latex Mexican wrestler's mask that I picked up in Odessa yesterday, then head out through the scraggly chapparal in the direction of the lab.

The darkness is so complete I can't even see my hand in front of my face, but I'm not stupid enough to start waving around a flashlight and announce my presence to all of creation, either. I slip on my goggles and press a little button on one side, and immediately my surroundings spring to life in a ghostly green glow. It's not pretty but it's enough to keep me from falling onto my face on the uneven ground.

I could be stone-cold blind, though, and still find the Meth lab just by following the stench. About a quarter-mile in from the service road an unholy combination odour of cat urine and rotten eggs assaults me as I top a low rise, and then I spot the eerie glow of a tiny hut sitting on the plain before me. As soon as I see it I drop to my stomach on the ground and focus in on it with my glasses. A little part of my brain worries about scorpions crawling into my pant legs, but that's just a chance I'll have to take. I don't intend to spend a long time here.

Tucked between two small hills above the backside of the arroyo Red told me about is a small pre-fab hut, like the kind on display in the parking lots at Home Depot. I can see a strange reflection coming off the roof, and it has me puzzled until I realise it's a large solar panel. A long dark shape that looks like a small stone wall is pressed up against one side of the hut, and I figure it must be a bank of car batteries used to store the juice from the solar panel. It's unlikely that could power a decent air conditioning unit, though, and I shudder to think how hot it must get in the hut during the day.

A little whirring fan unit on the roof is frantically spinning away, venting out toxic fumes. It looks like there are two windows built into the hut and both are covered over with something but not perfectly, and light is leaking out of each of them onto the ground around the hut, spreading out from the little shed like gangrene from an infected wound. All of the scrub within several feet is burned and eaten away, the consequence of being in the path of toxic chemicals dumped right onto the ground.

I scan the outside of the hut as carefully as I can and spot two camera units, one trained on the path leading to the main road, and the other pointed toward the arroyo behind the hut. The ruts leading up to the shack are well-worn enough for me to conclude there are no trip wires over them, and I figure the dealer must be counting on purely the physical isolation of his operation to provide him with security. There's a shiny new pickup parked at the end of the ruts, with gallon jugs of liquid sitting in its bed.

Excruciatingly slowly, I pick my way down from the little rise where I'd been laying and make my way over to the lab, staying in the cameras' blind spots. I lower each of my feet carefully as I step closer, and crane my neck listening for any sounds coming from inside. Once in a while I hear what might be the clink of glass on glass, but otherwise it's perfectly silent. I move to the hinge side of the hut's door. When it opens, I'll be behind it. There's a window right next to the door and I take up my place beside it, putting it between me and the door.

When I'm finally pressed-up against the hut, I remove my goggles and pull the wrestler's mask down over my head. I made sure when I bought it to pick out the nastiest, most grotesque creation on the shelf, and I chuckle to think what a horrific apparition I must make in the desert night. Pulling on the work gloves, I test their grip on the baseball bat, giving it a couple of practice swings like a ball player warming up in the batter's box. The swish of the bat as I whip it around in the air is a satisfying sound.

I wasn't lying when I told Jenny that I abhor physical violence, but an adventurous life has taught me that sometimes a judicious deviation from the rules can be the most efficient means of avoiding much more unpleasant complications.

Time to get this show on the road. Bending over, I pick up a handful of dirt and pebbles and very carefully toss some of it against the base of the hut's door. When it hits it rattles a lot more than I had been expecting. After listening to nothing but my own breathing for the last thirty minutes, the noise sounds like an avalanche.

I can almost taste the alert stillness that overtakes the interior of the hut. Counting to twenty, I wait just long enough to let the ears inside the hut strain to detect any other sound, then I toss a bit more dirt against the bottom of the door.

That gets a reaction. I hear a chair being pushed back, then the glow bleeding from the covered-over windows blinks out. Shuffling footsteps move closer to the wall where I crouch. Suddenly, without warning, the covering over the window beside me is yanked back and a blinding shaft of light sweeps out and pans across the landscape. I almost have to do a back flip to keep from being caught in the beam, but I'm close enough to the wall that the light doesn't catch me, and I press against the hut while the light paints the ground and hills across from me. I'm glad I took off my night vision goggles, or I'd be staggering around right now pressing my palms over a pair of seared optic nerves.

After about twenty seconds the light goes out and the window covering falls back into place, and I can hear the footsteps shuffling across the space. I throw another small handful of dirt against the base of the door.

"Son of a bitch!" comes from inside the hut. The lights stay off but the footsteps start moving again, and I hear a rattle from the direction of the door. I hear the click of the spotlight and see a white line glowing around the door frame.

"Fucking armadillos," mutters the voice, and very slowly the door opens outward, just the tiniest crack that very slowly gets wider. The light from the spotlight paints the ground in a progressively larger triangle as the door swings out.

The hand holding the spotlight comes into view first, followed by another hand, this one holding a gun, and then gradually the profile of a face edges into sight, craning forward and squinting down at the ground.

I've already set my stance, and I bring one foot out ahead of me and lean into it as I bring the bat round in a wide, sweeping arc, and swing for the fences. The bat impacts with both the forehead and the edge of the door, sending the latter crashing back against the face behind it and mashing the skull into the door frame. Both the spotlight and the gun clatter to the ground. I don't wait to admire the results of my work but instead step forward around the door which is wobbling back open. The figure in front of me has sunk to its knees in the dirt just past the door's threshold, and I lower my angle of swing and send another grand slam into the stands. There's a satisfying *thwack!* as the form in front of me is almost lifted into the air by the impact of my blow. It crashes against the half-open door then collapses forward onto the dirt, where it lays face down and doesn't move.

I'm not worried that I've killed him. I've seen enough people beaten to within an inch of their lives to know how much abuse the human body can take. I've probably given him a concussion and broken his jaw, maybe knocked out several teeth, but nothing that some wire and a couple weeks' bedrest won't cure. I pick up his gun and hurl it away as far as I can into the night. Then I retrieve the spotlight and quickly inspect the interior of the hut. I'm choking on the toxic fumes in the air and fighting not to vomit from the stench, and I make a mental note to bring along a gas mask if I should ever try something like this again. There are cans and bottles and hoses throughout the hut, an electric hotplate and countless jugs of water and various other liquids – benzene, isopropyl alcohol, iodine, lye, ammonia – a veritable cornucopia of toxic and extremely combustible chemicals, all packed into one ten-by-fifteen prefab hut.

What I see next, though, makes me freeze in my tracks and my blood run cold.

Sitting off to the side on a makeshift shelf is a large clear plastic storage bin, the kind you can pick up at Walmart for a few bucks. One half of it is filled to the brim with stacks of quart-size ziplock bags holding chunky white powder, and the other half is filled with shrink-wrapped bricks of hundred-dollar bills.

I immediately realise this is not merely a run-of-the-mill Meth lab, but a local distribution point, as well. The bin holds not just the product from this lab but the proceeds of the sales from probably half a dozen counties in this area. And judging from the fullness of the bin, it's overdue for a pickup.

I'm trying not to panic, but I can feel a tightness in my chest and my breathing gets a little shorter. Boxes like this don't just sit around for days waiting for someone to come pick them up. Either the scumbag who works in the lab was about to load this into his truck and deliver it to his overlords, or someone is on their way over here right now to collect it. I check my watch: it's a few minutes past midnight. With luck, maybe if I hurry I can beat it the hell out of here without making any new friends.

Working double-time now, I hustle back outside and stride over to each of the surveillance cameras and, standing out of the range of view, smash each of them into pieces with the baseball bat. I move back into the hut and grab the plastic bin and run over to the pickup parked beside the hut. I lower the bin over the side and into the truck bed and hustle over to the cab. The keys are in the ignition. Perfect.

A quick check of the jugs of liquid in the truck bed tells me that there are several large bottles of isopropyl alcohol, an equal number of jugs of benzene, and a large bottle of chloroform. Mr. Lab Tech must have just completed a supply run – this is not the sort of material one would leave sitting outside in the hot sun all day.

I start up the truck and spin it in a circle and drive it a safe distance past the hut, then leave it idling pointed toward the road. The scumbag is still laying where I dropped him, but he's starting to move around. He's probably high on his own product and might not even completely feel the effects of my work yet. I drag him by his collar across the scrub and dirt and he barely flinches, although every so often he lets loose a groan. He leaves in the wake of his passage a long trail of blood on the dirt. I leave him lying face down in a narrow depression behind a small boulder and hustle back to the lab.

Inside, I spot a small heap of filthy cloths piled on the floor in a corner, and I stuff them into a black plastic garbage bag I pull off a shelf. Running outside, I move away about twenty feet and scan the ground until I spot a large flat rock, about the size of a loaf of bread. I drop the rock into the garbage bag, pull a disposable Bic lighter from my pocket and light the rags on fire. Whatever they are stained with must like to burn, because they flare up immediately. Without pausing, I straighten up, grab the bag and heft it into the air, then swing it round like I'm competing in the hammer throw at the Olympics. I don't want to give the rags time to burn through the garbage bag so I immediately launch it through the air and watch it sail in a long, shallow arc right through the open doorway of the hut, where it plunges like a fiery comet right into the middle of the chaos of tubes and beakers and fluids.

The sound of breaking glass is immediately swallowed up by the ear-shattering roar of the lab exploding, and then by a louder salvo that actually shakes the earth as the bank of batteries beside the hut erupts in a massive detonation. If I hadn't thrown myself face down into a shallow ditch right after launching the bag, I would have been knocked back several feet by the force of the blast. Tucked beneath the lip of the ditch, though, covering my head with my hands, I feel only a slight battering from the scorching blast of air that bursts from the direction of the lab. I wince and squint my eyes shut as the ground around me is peppered with tiny bits of glass, wood, shattered plastic and various other debris. The air is full of glowing embers and I smell burning latex from the places where they have fallen onto the wrestler's hood that I'm still wearing.

When the downpour ends I pick myself off the ground and run as quickly as I can to the truck and leap into the cab, then gun the motor and drive off. When I hit the road I turn right and drive directly up to my car, pulling off the road and killing the truck lights. I pop my car's trunk and heft into it the plastic bin full of Meth and money, along with the wrestler's mask and my work gloves and goggles, then grab the jugs of chemicals and stuff as many of them as I can into the trunk and set the remainder on the back seat. The baseball bat I left at the scene. The methhead can keep it as a souvenir. I have no problem seeing what I'm doing as the sky behind me is bright orange and shedding lots of light, and I figure the blaze is still going strong. Without waiting another moment, I leap into my car and pull round the mesquite bush, then head back onto the road and speed away. I need to get to Interstate Highway 10 as soon as possible – the last thing I want is to meet another set of headlights on a deserted road with a burning Meth lab behind me.

My heart doesn't stop pumping until I hit an access point to I-10, where I force myself to calm down and drive at a leisurely pace. Within about five minutes I see a group of emergency vehicles on the other side of the highway speeding towards me, lights blazing and racing for all get-out in the general direction of the ex-lab. With all the oil derricks, storage tanks, oilfield servicing equipment and substations in this area, the oil companies maintain a close watch. The explosion and subsequent blaze must have lit up their monitoring stations like little Christmas trees. They'll be pissed when they get there and see the demolished Meth lab, but at least they'll have a perp to take out their anger on. They shouldn't have much trouble putting out any little fires around the lab, either; the desert around the hut is so barren there's not much to burn.

My night isn't quite over, though, as there's no chance in hell I'm leaving all this incriminating evidence in my car for even five minutes longer than I have to. I make a long loop to the south and east before turning off onto a small farm road which eventually leads me to an almost-invisible turnoff that you would miss if you weren't looking and already knew exactly where to find it. I bounce along for a few minutes then turn off the dirt track and drive up to a small rusted storage shed. When I get out of my car I'm briefly shocked at how exhausted I feel, a consequence of the night's work and a depletion of the adrenaline that coursed through my system for about an hour. Moving like the walking dead, I slowly and painfully carry the bin of money and Meth into the shed, then retrieve the jugs of chemicals and carefully lower them into an old rusted oil drum that's sitting abandoned behind the little hut. I pull out a Taser and a brand-new padlock from the glove compartment of my car and tuck the Taser into the bin and cover it with the ziplocks and money, then attach the padlock to the rusted hasp on the door and lock it.

On the way back home I make a detour to a Pilot Travel Center on I-285 on the road to New Mexico, and wash my car down until every speck of Texas clay and chaparral are nothing but a bad memory. I roll back into town just before sunrise, and gratefully climb up the back stairs from my parking space behind the pharmacy, tear off my stinking clothes and throw them onto the floor, and fall into bed.

willie

WAKE UP six hours later and open my eyes, and I'm looking directly at Jenny's rear end as she bends over at my bureau putting something into the bottom drawer. She's changed into a pair of white tennis shorts she must have found buried somewhere in my closet; I haven't played tennis in at least ten years. The shorts look better on her than they ever did on me. Her bottom is perfectly defined by the flimsy material, which stretches tight as she leans forward over the drawer. It's the best sight I can recall ever waking up to.

She straightens up and turns around in my direction and notices I'm awake.

"Oh, I'm so sorry, I tried to be quiet. I didn't want to wake you. I'm so sorry." This girl is always apologizing to me. She's going to give me a complex if she keeps it up.

"I had to wake up eventually, and I'm pretty sure you didn't do it. Just how long do you think a person can sleep, anyways?" I ask, looking at the clock that says it's well past noon.

Jenny laughs, a tinkling, musical giggle that probably qualifies as the nicest sound this room has heard since I moved in; this day keeps setting records. I realise that it's also the first time I've heard her laugh, and I'm happy that she's relaxing. She's a completely different person today than what I saw yesterday.

"Well, you were out pretty late," she says. "I heard you come in. You haven't been sleeping that long."

"Six hours is plenty for me, especially when it stretches into the afternoon. What were you doing just now? Were you looking for a piece of clothing?"

"No, I was putting some away. Your clothes absolutely reeked – I could smell them right through your closed door and into the other room. I washed them. You *do* know that you have a little washer and dryer in this place, don't you? They look like they've never been used before. I found an old box of detergent on a shelf beside them, but the powder has turned to a solid block. I had to cut off a chunk with a knife."

"I'm more into supporting our nation's struggling service industries. I take my clothes to a wash-and-fold operation in Pecos every week or so."

"What a waste! Honestly, men and laundry – it never fails

to puzzle me how such a simple task can intimidate even the most capable members of your sex."

"You can talk to me about that the next time you need to kill a spider," I say, sitting up in bed and swinging my feet to the floor. "But for now, I need to get dressed, so you're going to have to vamoose."

"OK, but I absolutely forbid you to put back on that t-shirt you wore last night – it's full of tiny burn holes in the back. God knows how you managed a trick like that. Were you standing with your back to a bonfire? Never mind, it doesn't matter. After I washed the stink out of it I put it under the bathroom sink with a bunch of other rags I found there. Oh, I'm sorry. You want to get dressed. Oops."
And she finally stops rattling along a mile a minute and sweeps out of my room and pulls the door shut behind her.

After a long leisurely shower, I'm having a late breakfast and Jenny is having a late lunch. I'm still just the tiniest bit groggy, and I let my eyes settle on the gleaming tines of her fork, following their passage from her plate to her mouth, and meditatively watching her lips close around the fork, and then watching it again as it repeats the journey back to plate and again to mouth.

If Jenny notices me watching her eat she doesn't say anything about it. She's full of energy and stored up conversation, chattering away nonstop, pausing briefly to eat little mouthfuls, then launching back into her monologue while I sip my coffee and watch her. Jenny has apparently cracked the coffee code and has brewed a pot that's every bit as good as the best I've had at the *Early Riser*. More and more I'm dreading the moment this job is done and she can go back to her farmhouse.

"Do you think I can have my phone back now?" asks Jenny as she gets up and starts clearing away our dishes.

"Um, I guess I should tell you, I don't have it anymore. It's hitching a ride in a pickup truck along with a trailer full of goats on its way to California."

"California?! What?"

"Remember the postcard of Venice Beach I had you fill out before I went to move your car?"

"Yes… but what's that got to do with my phone?"

"Well, I dropped them both into a bag that I gave to my friend Jorge. His cousin is driving them to Los Angeles as we speak. When he gets there, he'll make some local calls with your phone, to a couple of restaurants and some tourist attractions, and he'll drop your postcard in the mail, too."

"But what about my phone?!"

"That's coming back the same way it got there. Jorge's cousin should be back in town five or six days from now. You'll have to wait till then."

"But why such cloak-and-dagger stuff?"

"You told me Willie is related to the Sheriff. Just in case there's any poking around, I want it to look like you drove out west and back for a quick break."

As soon as I bring up Willie she becomes serious, as though her brain threw a switch. The light in her eyes dims a bit and her cheeks relax from the perpetual smile they have been maintaining since I woke up.

In for a penny, in for a pound, I think, and I start to tease out of her the details I'll need. She doesn't have a photo of him. I had hoped she'd snapped something once on her phone of him and her husband that I could retrieve from the Cloud, but apparently she was never motivated to preserve his image for posterity. Her description is mean-spirited and petty, but I try to glean the essential details nonetheless.

"You need to watch yourself around him," she tells me, looking like she's about to start up again on that lip-biting thing of hers. "He looks pathetic, but he's a snake. Don't turn your back on him, and don't underestimate him either. He'll do anything he thinks he can get away with. Your life might be in danger."

"Would he actually kill someone? It's a big step to go from being a scumbag to being a murderer. Not everyone has the guts for it."

"I'm pretty sure he's already crossed that line. I overheard a snippet of conversation he had with Marty once. Marty wouldn't tell me afterwards what they were talking about, but I thought I heard something about a 'body' and then later about moving something to where it couldn't be found."

"Well, thanks for the heads-up, but if it's any comfort to you, I wasn't about to turn my back on him anyways. I know too many good guys who've made that kind of mistake, and unfortunately it's a mistake you end up making only once. Now tell me where he lives. I'll need to go to his home."

Willie's not from our town – he lives by himself in a run-down ancient sharecropper's shack he inherited from his parents, stuck in the middle of the no-man's-land between Pecos and Fort Davis, about an hour south of us. The land there is so barren it makes our township look like the Garden of Eden. They can't grow any crops, there's nothing for cattle to graze on, and even the oil companies don't bother trying to suck anything out of the ground. It's no stretch of the imagination to figure out what might have motivated Willie to try out a career in the Meth industry.

According to Jenny, Willie splits his leisure time between a couple of run-down icehouses festering along Highway 20 about a half-hour south of us. I tell her I'll go see him tonight, and have her give me the best directions she can to his shack, then I help her finish clearing the table. Within a few minutes of joining me at the sink washing the breakfast dishes she's back to her chipper, upbeat self.

We spend the afternoon and early evening watching movies and playing Scrabble. At one point while we're watching TV Jenny falls asleep and leans against me with her head against my shoulder. I need to get up to pee but sit there for the next half hour crossing my legs until she wakes up and sits up straight.

Eventually it's time for me to leave. I want to get to Willie's place before it's dark out.

I'm going through the standard lecture about staying put when she surprises me by rising up on her tiptoes to give me a quick kiss on the mouth and tells me to be careful. I don't know if I looked shocked or not, but Jenny doesn't give me any time to feel awkward because she immediately turns on her heel and heads off to take a shower.

I drive directly to my little shack off the abandoned farm road and pull a couple of the shrink-wrapped bricks of currency out of the plastic bin, along with a handful of ziplocks of Meth. I tuck them away out of sight in a corner of my car's trunk – wouldn't want a random traffic stop to turn ugly.

Finding the shack where Willie lives is easier than I thought it would be. I drive south for about an hour along a beaten-up asphalt road that has more potholes than paving, then cross over I-10, and the farther I drive the more barren it gets. There are precious few living dwellings in the area, and the one detail Jenny could remember from the single time she'd stopped there with her husband was that it was about two miles down a dirt road running past an abandoned church.

I can see the church building from a distance, when I'm still at least two or three miles away, its bulky center tower and spire thrusting up into the endless sky like huge fat hand giving the finger to the universe. As I get closer I can see that the faded wooden siding is partly rotted and falling away in parts, creating gaping holes that reveal the walls' spines, a vertical tracery of ancient two-by-fours stubbornly refusing to collapse and let the structure die a dignified death. A wide sign hanging slightly askew displays simply the words "Christian Church", a generic, one-size-fits-all description that somehow makes the obsolescence of the former house of worship all the more tragic. Once again I think, *sic transit gloria mundi.* This time it seems a whole lot more appropriate.

I turn west onto a dirt track running away from the church, and about five minutes down it I come upon the only manmade structure I've seen since the church. To call it a shack would be insulting shacks everywhere in the world. But it's definitely inhabited, as the ruts leading up to the front porch are clear of any weeds or other plant growth. At the moment it's dark and deserted, slumping abjectly in the middle of a half-acre of scrub that would have to be specially bred to rise to the level of being called weeds. If the colour grey exists in nature, this property defines it. There's no living creature anywhere in sight. Even the birds must avoid this place.

I see no power lines leading to the shack, and I'm sure there's no generator on the property, which means that kerosene lanterns are the operative means of illumination. No wonder Willie spends his evenings in the icehouse.

I have no interest in the shack, and get out of my car and head over to a shed peeking out from behind the main building. It actually looks more inviting than the house, and appears to be only about ten or fifteen years old. Probably purchased and assembled sometime after Willie inherited the property, buoyed by hope and dreams of a brighter future.

The shed's door is slightly ajar and I grip it on the side, hoping there are no exposed rusty nails that will pierce my work gloves. The door pulls open reluctantly, mashing a path through the weeds that grow in front of it. I should have worn a hat. There's no telling what kind of creatures will drop down onto my head or fall under my collar from the dusty, spiderweb-covered roof struts. Gingerly I poke my head in and squint into the dim interior. There's grimy, rusting junk scattered haphazardly on the floor of the hut, along with a short stack of worn tires and a flimsy metal shelving unit leaning precariously away from the wall, holding a miscellaneous assortment of rusted tools and indistinct pieces of twisted metal. But at the end of one shelf is exactly what I was hoping for – an old, bent cardboard box with an oil company logo on its side and the words: "10W30 MOTOR OIL" and "12x1-QUART".

Wincing, hunched over, I gingerly take two steps into the shed, and when I'm close enough I grab the cardboard box and immediately retreat. Outside, I upend the box and out fall two empty plastic motor oil bottles and the desiccated corpse of a small spider. I fling the empty bottles back into the shed, ignore the dead spider, and hustle with the box over to my car. I have some rags in my trunk, and I pull them out and clean off the box as well as I can, then dig out the shrink-wrapped bricks of money and the ziplocks of Meth and throw them into the box, then hustle back to the shed, where I grit my teeth once again and step inside and carefully place the box back on the shelf, exactly where it was.

I step back and peer into the shed, admiring my work. It won't take Sherlock Holmes to spot the clean box shining away on the shelf among all the filthy debris.

I push and pull the door back and forth several times to mash down a good path over the weeds, then smudge my footprints in the dirt. I'm about to turn away to hustle back to my car when a strange glint catches my eye from around the corner of the shed. Curiosity gets the better of me and I move around the shed to find out what's causing the mysterious glimmer.

I'm not quite sure what to make of it. It's a wide, full-size mirror on a stand, very clean, looking like it's been polished very recently. There's a thick smudge of dark brown clay dirt mashed into its base, as though it had been standing upright outside. I bend down and touch the dirt and it feels fresh, but there's no dirt like that anywhere around this property. Evidently, the mirror has been placed here in the last few days, as the weeds underneath it haven't quite completely died. There's no other sign why it's out here.

Well, chalk it up as one of life's little mysteries, I've got no patience for puzzles right now. Maybe Willie salvaged it from a yard sale, although why he'd leave it out here hidden behind the shed I have no idea. I jump back in my car and back up through the ruts, then head up the road toward the church.

I still have a few hours to kill before I go see Willie. I want him to have a full night's drinking under his belt before we meet. I turn back north when I hit the church but don't cross over I-10 again, and instead I turn west onto a beat-up service road running parallel to the highway. I follow it until it comes alongside a gigantic truck stop on the highway, where a convenient access road lets me turn in and park.

A sign tells me that I'm now at the intersection where I-10 splits into the two main east-west arteries that run across Texas. Forking off to the northeast is I-20, which leads to Dallas-Fort Worth and five more southern states all the way to South Carolina, while I-10 continues its eastern journey along a more southern route, through Houston and along the Gulf coast right up to the Atlantic Ocean. In the other direction it continues west from here for another 80 miles or so before angling north and running parallel to the Mexican border right up to El Paso. Eventually it takes over part of the route once followed by the famous Highway 66, before meeting its glorious terminus at the Santa Monica Pier. Probably the same road Jenny's phone is taking on its trip to California.

It's a natural place for a truck stop, and the parking lot is filled with a couple dozen 18-wheelers, all thrumming along in a low thunderous rumble as their masters unwind inside the huge diner, steeling themselves for another long night of midnight travel. It's the perfect spot to kill a couple of hours in perfect anonymity, and I park with the other cars and walk into the restaurant, where I slip into a booth by the window and order my dinner.

For the next two and a half hours I sit watching through the plate glass as every segment of society passes through the truck stop parking lot: long-haul truckers carrying everything known to man, short-haul trucks carrying fruits and vegetables, cars full of tourists and pickup trucks full of farm workers, and maybe even the occasional oil millionaire who'd rather drive than fly, heading up to El Paso or over to Houston.

They wander inside, to eat at the diner or to pick up a snack in the convenience store or maybe just to pay for their gas, all of them walking slowly and stiffly, shaking out their legs as they stagger out of their vehicles, stretching and bending away the stiff muscles tortured by the long immobility of the drive. The only people seemingly not affected are the kids, who run and scatter across the hot asphalt as though they're dashing through a playground for recess, full of spit and vinegar, happy to be out of the car, happy to be on vacation, happy to be up late, happy to be anywhere but stuck at home.

When I finally tear myself away from the human comedy I'm almost sad to go, unwilling to reenter a world where people carry hidden agendas behind their eyes, where words have coded meanings and no one admits to what they really want. The fatigue of the truck stop is brutal in its unadulterated honesty, where people are reduced to their core components and simple needs. When I drive away the waning glow of the station's lights seem to represent a lost innocence that is slowly extinguished as I move back into the real world.

*   *   *

I get lucky and find Willie in the first place I look.

It's a squat, grey, unpainted cinder-block one-storey abomination of a building, slumping forlornly off by itself on a barren stretch of the Interstate service road a couple of miles outside a small collection of buildings that shouldn't have the nerve to call itself a town. A flickering fluorescent sign perches precariously above a shuttered window on the front, announcing the ready availability inside of Budweiser, "King of Beers". It also advertises the establishment's name of "The Cotton Club" – which seems to me to be a decidedly bold and ambitious choice by the owner, reminding me of the seedy, decrepit 8-unit motels scattered throughout the American hinterlands with names such as "Park Lane" and "The Plaza".

Undoubtedly the owner of this Cotton Club wasn't seeking to recreate the Black jazz mecca of New York's Harlem District, but rather aiming at channeling the area's farming community and their mainstay crop. Either way, the establishment looks like it is failing on all fronts, much like several of the beat-up pickup trucks haphazardly strewn in the front lot. They're scattered randomly in the lot, as though a skyscraper-sized child had been playing with them and left them just as they were when his mother called him in for dinner.

From the outside the place looks like a seedy, disreputable dump, with overflowing garbage cans spilling into an oil-stained dirt parking lot peppered with basketball-sized potholes. On the inside it's exactly what the outside promised.

I open the door and almost reel backwards as I am punched in the face with the stench of stale beer and sweat. A thick fog bank of cigarette smoke hangs low in the air, creating eerie pillars of light oozing down from several pot lights in the ceiling. Scattered tables of small groups of men punctuate the room, little islands of shadowy shapes that I pass by on my way to the bar at the far wall.

Willie isn't hard to spot. He is all alone at the bar, sitting hunched over, dead eyes staring into a half-empty glass of beer sweating on the bar in front of him.

I had thought that Jenny was being malicious when she described Willie to me, but once I get close to him I see she was being kind. The first thing I notice is his sallow skin, a greasy, pasty, pock-marked mask that would make a jaundice sufferer look hale and hearty in comparison. His sunken eyes are little more than holes in his head where reflected light goes to die, hiding behind a clump of stringy, matted hair that clings feverishly to his scalp and oozes onto his narrow rounded shoulders.

Willie is gripping the glass of beer in one of his hands, and I notice the thick dark mass of dirt under his overgrown, chipped nails. None of them are the same length and most show signs of having been chewed off. There's a smell emanating from him that is reminiscent of a dying animal, with the added flavours of rotten eggs and urine thrown into the mix. It's seeping out either from his body or from his clothing, a baggy camouflage jacket and pants combination which looks like it was last washed sometime around the Reagan administration.

He doesn't look up when I sit down on the bar stool next to him. I don't imagine he is in the mood to be making new friends. It's probably so long since that last happened he likely doesn't remember how it's done, anyways.

"Bud," I say to the bartender, proving that advertising really does work. When I have it in my hand and the bartender has moved back to the other end of the bar, I say quietly, to no one in particular, "I hear you're the man to see around here for some product."

Willie makes no response at all.

"I'm mostly interested in my friend Christina," I try again, using the popular nickname around these parts for Meth.

That brings Willie out of his Silent Sam impression and he murmurs quietly, "Maybe I was someone who could help you out before, but you're too late, pal. I'm out of the game. I got nothing for you."

"Just what I was hoping," I reply. "I'm not looking to buy – I need someone who can move some supply."

"You're still out of luck, mister. I'm all out of cash, too. After I pay for this drink I'd have a hard time even coming up with bus fare."

"Still not a problem," I say. "From what I hear, your credit is just fine. I'm happy to wait for my payment until after you move the inventory."

He finally turns his head to look at me, then. He stares a little longer than might normally be considered polite in most social circles, but I think he uses up at least half the time in trying to focus his eyes. When he speaks again he sounds almost thoughtful.

"So you're my fairy godmother, are you? Come down from the clouds to dump a load of treasure into my arms? How stupid do you think I am, copper?"

"The more you talk, even stupider than I thought before. Or haven't you ever heard of 'entrapment'? And what makes you think a small-time nobody like you would be worth wasting valuable law enforcement resources on? Just how much do you think of yourself anyways, loser?"

If he were just a little bit sober that might have been enough to provoke him to take a swing at me, but the miracle of alcohol keeps him on his stool long enough for him to start considering the offer I'm dangling before him.

"Look," I say, "This isn't a complicated proposal. I've got product. You've got customers. Sounds to me like these two puzzle pieces go together. It's not rocket science."

"How much do you have," he asks, as the implications of my proposition begin to work their way through his fried cerebral cortex.

"Enough to keep this shithole of a county high for the next month. More if things go well."

"You connected?" he asks warily. Even walking turds like Willie know better than to lay down in bed with the Mob if they can avoid it. He'd heard the stories of good ol' boys found with their balls stuffed down their throats and their hands chopped off. And then there are the stories of the Mexican cartels, which are a whole new level of brutality all on their own.

I shake my head "no".

"I'm an independent operator, Willie. That's why I've come to you. Manufacturing the stuff's not a problem, but I've got no customer base. I figure maybe there's room in your distribution network for a little increased supply."

"What the fuck you mean, 'distribution network'? Who do you think you're dealing with here? I got a list of wetbacks and dead-end dirt farmers. It don't go much farther than that. Maybe your occasional high school student, but aside from jackrabbits, that about sums up my 'distribution network'."

"Look, Willie, I didn't come here to argue. Are you interested or not? I've got a bin full of the stuff in a shed about five miles from here. I can put it in your hands tonight and be back in a week to collect my payment. Or I can get in my car and drive to the next wide spot in the road and get the next guy to take me up on my offer. It's your choice."

Willie wets his lips with his tongue. We both know he needs this, but the uncanny coincidence of my showing up at precisely the right moment is holding him back from jumping into my arms like a long-lost brother. He's frozen in indecision and sits there in silence.

"Well, I guess that's what I'll do then, Willie. Sorry to bother you." I toss a ten-spot onto the bar. "Thanks for your time – your beer's on me. Wouldn't want you to come up short on that bus fare and have to walk home."

I nod at the bartender and motion that I'm paying for both of us, and I stand up to leave. But my feet don't even hit the floor before Willie says, "OK. Alright. I'm in. Let's go get your stuff."

*   *   *

I make Willie follow me in his pickup truck. Our two vehicles bounce and rattle their way down the old gravel farm road I drove down yesterday, twin pairs of yellowed high-beams painting dancing firehoses of light through the pitch-black Texas night.

The rear shocks in my old sedan stopped providing any semblance of cushioning at least a decade ago and the car's back end leaps into the air with each hump in the dirt track. I glance at Willie's headlights gyrating and leaping in my rearview mirror and figure his truck is in even worse shape. I hope he doesn't throw out an axle before we get to where we're going, and I slow down a bit more to avoid any excessive jostling.

The dirt and weeds that come to life in the sudden illumination of my headlights are punctuated occasionally by pairs of tiny shining pinpricks gleaming in the dark of the night; eventually the beams come close enough to reveal the shape of alert jackrabbits, possums, and armadillos, nocturnal shoppers annoyed to have their evening foraging interrupted by my noisy passage through their open-air supermarket. A dark blob on the right side of my windshield has me momentarily puzzled until the moonlight reveals it to be an assassin bug taking a leisurely break on the glass, where it perches contentedly until a particularly rough bounce sends it, too, skittering away into the night.

An indistinct form slowly takes shape in the field to my right, and I turn onto a pair of ruts worn into the dirt and drive up to the small rusted metal hut, where my brand-new shiny metal padlock hangs enticingly from the brown hasp on the door.

I pull up to the hut and leave my headlights shining at the door. Willie rattles up to me and settles to a stop just behind my car. He turns off his engine and after about ten seconds it agrees to quit running, stubbornly popping and sputtering and sighing until it settles into a noisily clicking, hissing hulk. I'm starting to feel like a millionaire in my comparatively palatial sedan.

Willie tumbles down from his truck, pushing his hair back from his face and stumbling up to me in the dark.

He probably thinks I can't tell he has a gun tucked into the waistband at the back of his pants, but the way he's careful sliding out of the truck and then self-consciously adjusting the dirty t-shirt that hangs loose over his pants is a dead giveaway.

I make sure to turn my back to him and to lean over in the dirt to fiddle for a second with my shoe so he can see I obviously sport no similar sidearms, and then I straighten up and unlock the rusty door.

The hut is just big enough to accommodate a four-wheeler dirt bike, but the only thing inside it is the plastic storage bin sitting smack-dab in the middle of the space. My car's high-beams spray light through the open door and onto the container bin, lighting it up like a solitary actor in a spotlight on a dark stage.

Willie tries to look calm, I've got to grant him that. But his breathing almost comes to a halt when he sees the bags of Meth and the stacks of currency next to them. There's no doubt in my mind that it's the most money he's ever seen in one place in his whole life. I can almost hear the wheels clicking in his head. His right hand makes a discreet movement and disappears behind his back. I know what's coming and head him off at the pass.

"Here, give me hand with this," I say. "Let's put it in your truck. I'll take the money and you can have the bin."

I pick up one end, and Willie brings his hand back out from behind him and picks up the other end.

"Shit. This fucker's heavy," says Willie, surprised at the heft of the box.

"S'ok, your truck's right here," I say, and take the lead, walking backwards and guiding him over to the bed of his pickup where I want him to be.

We lower the box over the side and Willie steps back as I straighten out the box and pat down the bags of meth inside it – after reaching in and extracting my Taser from under the ziplocks.

Suddenly, I see two glassy eyes staring at me from a lifeless face in the truck bed.

"What the f –" I recoil in surprise but Willie just laughs. A dead coyote is laying in the truck bed, sharp canines gleaming in the moonlight, swollen tongue lolling out between his open jaws. The fur is matted and dirty and smeared with dried blood, and a putrid odour wafts up from the corpse to assault my nostrils.

"Roadkill, dude," says Willie between chuckles. "I grab it whenever I can. Never know when it'll come in handy."

I still have my back to him and my hand in the darkness of the interior of the truck bed when I hear a telltale click behind me and turn to see Willie cocking a six-shooter and looking at me with a shit-eating grin on his face.

"How long," says Willie smugly as he sees my startled expression, "Do you think it will take for someone to find your body all the way out heeeeeeeeeeeeeeeeeeeeeeeeeeeeeeeeeeee –"

Willie's question breaks off into a keening, screeching wail as the needles from my Taser embed themselves in his chest, causing him to clench his fists and to squeeze off a blast from his cocked pistol, which roars to life and buries a round into the wheel well of his pickup, about four inches away from my left thigh.

The huge quantity of alcohol in Willie's system must be slightly dulling the effects of the Taser. He collapses slower than I would have expected, sinking to the ground like a human impersonation of a controlled building demolition, dropping first to his knees, then plopping his butt down onto his calves, then slumping over at the waist, before finally tumbling forward to twitch and jerk uncontrollably on the ground. I keep my finger pressed down on the trigger the whole time, of course. Extended shocks from a Taser can be dangerous for a person, but I'm not going to lose any sleep over Willie's health prognosis.

Once he's fully collapsed face-down in the dirt I release the trigger, then reach down and pick up his gun before hustling over to my car where I retrieve a roll of duct tape from the back seat. Working quickly before his temporary paralysis wears off, I tape up Willie's hands and arms behind his back and wrap his ankles as tightly as I can, then drag him around the truck and stand him up against it while I fumble open the passenger door.

Grunting with effort and wrinkling my nose against the stench of his now-urine-soaked clothing, I heft him into the passenger seat before closing the door.

Popping the trunk on my car, I pull out two five-gallon jugs of gasoline that I picked up at the truck stop, and empty both jugs into the gas tank in Willie's truck. It takes all of it. Just as I had suspected, Willie was driving on empty. I throw the empty jugs back into my trunk along with the Taser and all but three of the bricks of money from the bin, turn off my car's headlights and grab a stun gun from the glove box, then get into Willie's truck and slowly back us down the dirt track.

I know all the back roads leading to Odessa and I take them the whole way, going nice and slow, intent on avoiding any law enforcement looking to kill time between donut stops. It's not too long before Willie regains consciousness but he doesn't say a word, just half-sits, half-lies in his seat, leaning up against the door and glaring at me murderously.

"The boys in St. Louis don't like you operating in their territory, Willie," I say in a low monotone that I'm hoping will come across as both threatening and mysterious. "You can consider this a warning. The next one you won't even see coming."

Willie has no response to that, but stops glaring at me. Now he just looks frightened.

It's just coming up on 4am when we get to Odessa, and I know the stretch of Main Street I need and I drive directly there and pull to a stop on the deserted street across from a local jewelry store. There isn't another car or any living being anywhere in sight.

When I scouted out the town a couple of years ago it had taken me a long time to find a stretch of the commercial district with no cameras facing the street, and as far as I can tell this particular block is still nicely devoid of any electronic witnesses. I know there are cameras in the jewelry store, but my best inspections earlier had revealed none pointed at the street. It's not exactly Tiffany's, and the proprietor obviously is more concerned with shoplifting than teams of heist men driving up to carry off his inventory.

I open my door, step out into the street, then lean over into the truck and pull Willie over to the driver's side. Foolishly, he decides this is an opportune moment to start struggling, so I stick my stun gun up against his neck and hold down the trigger.

When his thrashing slows down I resume pulling him until he's in place behind the wheel. Not wasting any time, I grab the storage container and lug it up out of the truck bed and over to the cab.

I start scooping out the bags of Meth and piling them onto the passenger seat beside Willie. They make an impressive pile when I'm done, with some spilling onto the floor in front of the seat. Next, I take the three remaining shrink-wrapped bricks of money and toss them onto the Meth, then pull Willie's gun out from behind the seat where I'd stuck it earlier, wipe it clean and throw it onto the seat along with the money and bags of drugs.

Willie is still in pretty bad shape from the last jolt I gave him and doesn't move when I take out my pocket knife and reach down to slice the duct tape off his ankles, making sure to leave one of his feet resting limply on the gas pedal. Then I push him forward against the steering wheel and slice the tape off his wrists and arms. Once released, his arms flop forward but otherwise he doesn't move.

I shut the door then reach through the open window and shift the gear lever into "D", and the sputtering truck starts inching forward. Holding the steering wheel and trotting alongside the truck, I turn it hard to the left until it's heading diagonally across the street directly toward the jewelry store, and when I am sure the trajectory is true, I jam my stun gun into Willie's neck one last time and feed him another 50,000 volts of Edison's Best.

When the current hits Willie's nervous system his legs shoot straight out and his foot jams down onto the accelerator with the force of a pile driver. The truck bucks forward harder than I've seen it move all night, and I have just barely enough time to pull my arm back out before the vehicle rockets away.

Real life isn't like in the movies and as much as I would like to stand there calmly lighting up a stogie and watching the fireworks as the truck impacts with the plate glass window of the jewelry store, I am already running back across the street and bending down to pick up the storage bin when I hear the impact behind me, followed by the sound of sheets of broken glass hitting the sidewalk. A shrill little whooping alarm immediately starts shrieking from the direction of the store.

I run as quickly as I can down the street and around the corner into the nearest back alley, where I pick a random dumpster and throw the empty bin into it along with the strips of duct tape I cut off Willie, and then trot off into the night.

It's not much more than 30 seconds later that I hear the distant wail of approaching sirens. A bit of excitement for the Odessa P.D. night shift, I think. So much for break time, boys.

Twenty minutes later I am sitting in the passenger seat of a truck heading back towards my neck of the woods, courtesy of a friendly Mexican with a trailer full of hay that I'd met gassing up at the local Love's Travel Stop, only too happy to take 50 simoleons in exchange for the ride.

He thinks it's a little curious when I make him let me out in the middle of nowhere, but smiles and shakes my hand and says he'll see me around. I wait for him to disappear from view before I strike out across the field toward the little hut about a mile away, just behind a distant rise.

The sun is just peeking above the horizon when I get to my car and the hut. Bending down, I pull off the Missouri license plate that's covering my own, pop the trunk and pull out the bricks of money, and toss the lot into the oil drum behind the shed. All in all, I think, a good night's work.

domestic life

WAKE UP at noon again, but this time Jenny's tight little bottom is nowhere in sight. Grunting with effort, I drag myself out of bed and roll halfway onto the floor, then straighten up and groggily pull on a pair of sweatpants and a t-shirt. When I stagger into the kitchen following the heavenly aroma of Jenny's coffee, she's sitting there looking like a lottery ticket holder who's just heard the first five numbers of her ticket called and is watching the final ball about to drop from the cage.

She follows me with her eyes every step of the way as I shuffle over to the counter, grab a cup, fill it with java, open the fridge, pull out the cream and splash it into my cup, then replace the carton and close the fridge door. I can't swear to it but I don't think she's even blinked since I came in sight, and she says nothing as I stumble over to the table and slide down onto a chair.

"It's done." I say, finally breaking the silence. "Willie won't be back. Ever."

She exhales in a loud burst. She must have even been holding her breath. Her relief is tangible, but there's a sudden concern that fills her face.

"You didn't – that is I mean, he isn't –"

"No, he's not dead. But he's not coming back, either."

"Then how –"

"The State of Texas will generously be providing Willie with full room and board, complete with three square meals a day, for the foreseeable future. For about 8 to 10 years, in fact, if I had to make a guess."

"Eight to ten years?"

"If that's still the recommended time for being caught with a large quantity of illegal drugs, money and a firearm, which I believe it is."

She doesn't say anything, she just launches herself out of her chair and onto me, laughing and peppering me with kisses and hugging me tightly.

"Hey hey, watch the coffee," I say, but I'm hugging her back and neither one of us is letting go.

*   *   *

As much as I would like to lock myself away all day in my apartment with Jenny, appearances have to be maintained.

I can't risk some alert observer noticing that the two of us seem to be missing at exactly the same time. And so, despite having breakfasted quite well, I wander down to the *Early Riser* and force myself to eat a turkey club sandwich. Sadly, Renault's coffee is a distant second to Jenny's. Coffee is Renault's only failing, in my opinion, a reflection of the decided lack of interest in gourmet coffee exhibited by the French people as a whole. Of all the countries in the world where I've lived, France has offered the most disappointing choices in coffee. If you want to discuss wine, that's a different story. But as far as coffee goes, they're a lost cause.

While I'm desultorily chewing away on my sandwich, I take the opportunity to innocently inquire of Renault if he's heard from Jenny. He stops rushing around the dining area long enough to wipe a bead of perspiration from his temple, then grimaces sadly, shaking his head. And then a call from the kitchen draws him away again, and I finish up, tossing a ten-spot onto the counter and slipping back out of the café.

I have some errands to run today and I perform them on autopilot, barely conscious of what I'm doing, as my thoughts keep returning to the beautiful girl who's sitting in my apartment waiting for me to return. At the filling station a rancher friend I bump into starts rattling on about some nest of assassin bugs he's found in a woodpile behind his barn. I make the appropriate "tsk-tsk" sounds every few moments, but my mind is on Jenny and his words are falling away like dead leaves blowing past me in the street, skittering away on the edge of my consciousness.

Finally, I bow to the unavoidable truth and give up on whatever other tasks I had laid out for myself today, and head directly for the Piggly Wiggly, where I pick up some steaks to bring home for our dinner. I'm on my way out the door when a bucket of cut flowers on display catches my eye and I go back and purchase them. The thought occurs to me that this is the first time in my life I've ever bought flowers for a girl, and it's simultaneously an unsettling and a thrilling revelation.

It's also a new feeling when I unlock my door and step into a home with someone inside waiting for me. She's there on the couch, looking over her shoulder expectantly, smiling from ear to ear, and suddenly all the day's events fragment into dust in my mind and are swept away. The face that had been hovering in my mind's eye all afternoon is suddenly now a tangible thing, replacing all my other concerns, priorities and distractions. She leaps up off the couch and grabs the flowers and coos delightedly and gives me a kiss and whirls away in search of a vase, while I stand pathetically in place, unsure of myself in my own home.

The dinner we eat and the movie we watch all blur away in my consciousness as I grapple with this unfamiliar situation, until finally I stumble off to bed and leave her curled up on the couch, snoozing under a blanket and wearing one of my old t-shirts and some baggy sweat pants.
I want to carry her off to my bed with me and wrap myself around her, listening to her breathe as I sink my face into her hair and slip off into peaceful sleep, but instead I lay down alone with nothing but the cold, mechanical ticking of my bedside clock to usher me into dreamland.

When I wake up the next morning I reflexively look over to my bureau, but still there's no girl there, no one bending over and tucking away my clothes, no delicious sight of forbidden fruit dangling before my eyes.

Yawning, I straighten up and adjust the sweatpants I slept in, futilely trying to arrange myself to lessen the obviousness of my morning tumescence before shuffling into the bathroom to pee. And coming face to face with Jenny.

She's standing at the mirror, wrapped in a large bath towel that barely makes it far enough down her body to protect her virtue. Her hair is hanging down in straight, wet strands; she is pulling a brush through it and tiny droplets of water escape from the tips and disappear into the fabric of the towel below.

She turns to face me when I come in and lights up the room with a hundred-watt smile. Her skin is glistening in just-showered dampness. The scent of vanilla fills the air while little wisps of steam swirl in gentle eddies under the pot lights in the ceiling.

"Good morning, babe," she says, and walks up to me and puts her hands on my shoulders and kisses me on the mouth. "Or is it afternoon? I've lost track. Doesn't matter, I'm sorry I'm still in here – I wanted to be done before you woke up. It's all yours now, though. I'm just finishing up."

I've got my hands on either side of her, holding her waist just above her hips, and I wonder what sort of superhuman willpower has overtaken me, to enable me to resist pulling off her towel on the spot and letting Nature take its course. But she doesn't leave me any time to grapple with the impulse, and moves around me and out the doorway and into the kitchen area.

"Now that you're up I'll make breakfast," she says, and with a twist she disappears into the privacy of my bedroom to get dressed, and the bathroom door slowly swings shut in her wake. I am left standing there at the sink, staring at the back of the closed door, and I still haven't said a word since I woke up.

The image of Jenny's shimmering form hovers a moment longer in my mind's eye, and I have to shake myself to come out of the little trance I've fallen into. At the back of my mind a thought tickles my brain stem, something that's bothering me about a picture that's not quite right, but it's too far out of reach to be of any use to me, and I leave it back there while I pull off my pants and step into the shower.

Twenty minutes later, showered, shaved, fully awake and sitting at the table, wolfing down a plateful of scrambled eggs and bacon, I figure Jenny must be one of those girls who have bought into the notion that the way to a man's heart is through his stomach, and I mumble grateful noises while she refills my coffee and plunks down a board of toast and jam beside my plate. She smiles at my efforts to talk through a full mouth and ruffles her fingers through my hair.

"Don't talk. Eat," she giggles. "You deserve it. Anything else I can do for you, just say the word."

"Don't tempt me," I grin up at her.

"Ha! I see my evil plan is working to perfection," she says, squeezing onto my lap and sitting sideways on my thighs and putting her arms around my neck. "Now if only I had some decent clothes to wear instead of your old castoff t-shirts and exercise pants, I could be a happy woman."

"Oh no, you don't. You're not buying your freedom with a simple plate of eggs and bacon—"

"Don't forget the toast."

"— And toast—"

"— And the coffee."

"— And coffee. And the answer is still 'no'. It will be at least three more days before your phone gets here, and you don't step foot outside this apartment before then.

Your postcard hasn't even arrived yet. And I'm pretty sure Willie hasn't so much as made it through processing by now. You're staying put until your alibi is rock solid."

"But hon, you can't seriously be thinking I'm going to walk around in your old clothes until then! If I don't get a proper change of clothes right soon I can't be held responsible for my actions."

She's got her head buried in the crook between my shoulder and neck, and I can feel my willpower melting away like an ice cream cone in a hot car.

"Pleeeeeeze, can't we do something? What if we wait until dark tonight, and then I scootch down really low in your car and you drive me to my house just long enough for me to pick up some essentials, then we can come right back and I won't make another peep about it until my phone gets here. Please, baby?"

A wise man knows when he's beat, and so do I. To tell the truth, I'm surprised I held out as long as I did.

After breakfast is all cleared away we retreat to the couch and end up spending the rest of the day there, reading, playing Scrabble, snoozing, curled up together and snacking on junk food. But the time passes quickly and once the clock strikes five Jenny starts peeking out the blinds every ten minutes checking to see if it's dark enough yet for us to reasonably slip out undetected, and it takes all my force of persuasion to keep her inside until at least a semblance of dusk has settled over the town. For once our community's economic downturn works in our favour as there are no random passersby to catch sight of us as we creep down the back stairs and slip into my car before heading out of town.

Her farm isn't far away. About five miles south of the city limits we turn left off a paved surface road onto a smooth band of gravel with slight washboarding only just starting to creep in. The last remaining rays from the setting sun behind us light up the trees and shrubs with an ethereal, golden glow, as though we're driving into an illuminated manuscript from a medieval text.

"One of the farmers who lives along this stretch has a small dairy operation," she tells me as we jiggle along. "He keeps the road smooth 'cause he doesn't like the milk jugs getting shook up too much when he takes them to the Market in Pecos. He has a small grader that he runs over it every couple of years or so."

"A dairy on this land? What do the cows graze on? Cactus?"

"He's got an arrangement with a fellow who grows alfalfa on a spread closer to the Guadalupe Mountains west of here. They get a bit of rain there, coming off the hills, enough to grow grass, at least. Everybody here trades with everyone else, it makes a lot more sense than taking pennies on the dollar from the mills and the middlemen."

"How did you and Marty end up here?"

"It used to be his parents' place. But they died and it went to his brother, but then he up and kicked the bucket, too, so it fell into Marty's hands. I think it took Marty by surprise. I don't believe he ever expected to end up actually owning the place and living here. I know I sure didn't."

I raise my eyebrows slightly and glance over at her. I can't tell if it's resentment I hear or the tired resignation voiced by so many of the long-term residents who are still holding on out of a sense of commitment to the land and their ancestors.

"It wasn't going to be this way," she continues, looking out the window at the parched scrub all around us. "I met Marty in El Paso when he was stationed at Fort Bliss and married him way too quickly.

"It's my fault he quit the service. I didn't want to wake up one day to the news he'd been cooked alive in his tank somewhere on the other side of the planet. I figured with the training the army gave him he could land a good job as a mechanic somewhere north of this open-air furnace, or maybe in California. Before we could make our escape, though, everything fell to shit and… well, here we are."

"I see," I say quietly.

"No, no, I mean here we are – turn right at the fence."

I slow down as we approach a two-board wood fence that runs off ahead and to the right, then we turn down a path consisting of two shallow ruts worn into the ground alongside the fence. There's nothing on the other side of the fence but weeds and cactus and bare ground. After a few hundred meters the ruts come to an end in a wide circle in front of a clapboard house facing north, sitting beside a majestic sprawling Cathedral Oak that looks to be about two hundred years old. A few Cedar Elms are growing in a tight clump at the opposite end of the house, huddled together looking like they're plotting to rise up and overthrow the Oak one day when it's not looking.

The fields stretching out around the house look fallow and barren. Yellow chaparral spreads out to the horizon, flecked with stubborn clumps of purple-green thistle and cheatgrass interspersed with the occasional patch of cactus.

The remnants of furrows appear here and there, indicating long-since abandoned attempts to cultivate the ground and produce a marketable crop.

The house is a pleasant-looking two-storey affair, well-tended and in good condition. It's obviously been painted within the last year and still has a nice shine on the side away from the sun. The ubiquitous rooster weathervane twists lazily on the roof while a couple of crows sit a few feet away, eyeing it suspiciously and daring it to try something. A deep, wide, raised wooden porch with a single white railing runs across the front of the house, where a couple of white wooden Adirondack chairs with a small low table between them sit expectantly in the shade of the Cathedral Oak.

"This is a nice-looking place, Jenny. What do you grow here?"

"Methamphetamine, apparently," she replies with a slight grimace.

It's been almost a month since Marty died and the yard immediately around the house is only just starting to show signs of neglect. A few weeds are creeping in alongside the base of the porch, and four or five tumbleweeds have collected into a small bundle herded up against the slanted roof of a root cellar poking out from the base of the house behind the oak tree.

"Where do you get your mail?" I ask, looking for a pile of unopened letters and flyers.

"There used to be a set of mailboxes back where we turned off the main road that runs south from town, but a drunk driver knocked the whole lot of them out of the ground about five years back. The people here decided to opt for free Post Office boxes the city was offering us. Hoping to lure more traffic into town, I suppose. Marty and I don't get much mail except for bills, so we don't pick up our mail more than once a week, usually."

She pauses for a minute and looks at the ground.

"I guess I'd better learn to stop talking as though he's going to pull up any minute in his beat-up old truck and walk up like everything's all normal. I just…."

Now it's my turn to be quiet and look at the ground. There's nothing for me to do but let her sort through it herself.

"Let's get this done," she says suddenly, and walks rapidly up a wide set of four steps cut into the front porch. The door is unlocked and she walks right in.

"You always go away and leave the place unlocked?"

"I expected to be back after seeing you. I didn't realize you were going to kidnap me," she says, grinning. "Besides, someone who wants in just has to break a window. It's not like anyone's close enough to hear. I'd rather have them come in without breaking anything."

She moves to flip a light switch but I grab her hand.

"No, I don't want to advertise our presence any more than we have to. The lights can be seen a long way off. Let's get what we need to and be gone before it's too dark to see."

I follow her up a wide stairway that creaks painfully beneath our feet. The light is better upstairs, with a few shafts of sunlight still bleeding in through the side windows of the master bedroom. Jenny hustles over to her closet to grab the clothing she needs while I head into the bathroom with a small duffel and start tossing in the toiletries she keeps on the counter.

I'm looking around for more likely items to include when something in the wastebasket catches my eye. I lean down and pull out a small plastic bag marked with the logo of a costume and party store in Odessa. Inside the bag is a receipt, dated for the day before Jenny came to see me.

"OK, that should do it," she calls out from the closet. "How are you making out in there?"

I stuff the receipt back in the bag and shove it back down into the wastebasket. When she pokes her head round the bathroom door I'm just finishing zipping up the duffel.

"I think I got everything you'll be needing," I say. "Are we done?"

"Yep. I'm an easy packer. This should keep me comfortable for the next week, if need be."

Her arms are full, holding what looks like the contents of a small clothing store against her chest. Her face is just visible above the pile of garments.

"An easy packer, eh?" I say. "I shudder to think what you take with you on vacation."

"I thought this *was* a vacation," she says, flashing me a mischievous smile. "Who needs Hawaii when we've got your couch?" And she heads off onto the landing and staggers carefully down the stairs. I quickly peek into her closet to see what's left and then follow her downstairs.

*   *   *

I suppose Jenny feels I deserve some sort of reward for letting her go out to her house against my better judgment, because the first thing she does once we get back to my apartment is to go into my bedroom and change into fresh clothing. If that's what you can call what she puts on, that is.

I'm bending over at the fridge, pulling out a couple of cold ones, when I straighten up and turn around to see her standing in the doorway wearing a tight, sheer white lace chemise held up by two thin spaghetti straps and finishing with a decorative wide lace hem at the bottom that just covers the top of her thighs. It conceals far, far less than it reveals, and what little it does conceal my imagination has absolutely no trouble filling in.

"Well," I croak, "I'm not sure if you're trying to tell me that we need to go back because you forgot to pick up any underwear…."

She doesn't say anything but instead gives me a dirty, throaty laugh, then walks up and drapes her arms around my neck. I can feel her body pressing against mine, and I fumble to put the beer bottles on the counter before they slip from my fingers.

"You know what I think?" she says, bringing her lips to within one inch of mine.

"Um… that I'm really overdressed right now?"

"No. More like I am," she says, and removes her arms from around my neck, then reaches her right hand over to her left shoulder and pulls the strap down and lets it droop down against her elbow.

I can't say anything in reply, as her tongue is in my mouth, so I let my fingers do the talking, and I reach up and pull the other strap down off her shoulder.

PART II

blowback

*"For they have sown the wind,
and they shall reap the whirlwind."*

Hosea 8:7

THE EARLY RISER CAFÉ

HE *EARLY RISER CAFÉ* is almost completely emptied-out, as the last of the morning stragglers finish up their coffees and wander reluctantly into the rising heat radiating off the parking lot. I check my watch and note with a grunt that it's almost 10am. Renault is already busy preparing for the lunch crowd, moving back and forth between the large walk-in refrigerators and the prep counter behind the big open cutout separating the dining area from the kitchen. Manuel is busy in the kitchen scraping the big grill, and Jenny is moving methodically from one table to another, clearing off dishes and wiping down the vinyl checkered tablecloths. She has a big smile on her face as she works, and it's clear she's happy to get out of my small apartment, notwithstanding the immense entertainment value of our recent activities.

We did our best in the past few days to break my bed, and I think we came close to succeeding. We were having such a good time we paid little attention to the arrival of Jenny's phone, and immediately turned it off and abandoned it on a side table for another four days while we explored the physical limits of our attraction to each other. We acted as though we had just invented sex and wanted to give it a thorough road test before sharing it with the rest of humanity.

When Jenny finally broke down and called Renault, telling him she could return to work today, she and I accepted the change in our routine as an almost necessary respite to stave off exhaustion. But now, watching her glide from table to table, I am amazed to reflect that my eyes are still drawn irresistibly to her little butt, her smooth, shapely legs, to the glistening wave of blonde locks that dangle around her shoulders. And Jenny, for her part, seems to feel similarly, glancing up from time to time to shoot me sexy, dirty glances, sticking out her tongue lasciviously or making puckering movements with her lips when she thinks no one is looking.

Renault staggers over to where I'm sitting, at a table on the far wall at the opposite end of the café from the door. He must be absolutely worn out from the last five hours of unceasing movement, ministering to the guests, assisting in the kitchen, cashing out the diners and welcoming new ones. And yet, paradoxically, he still seems to be brimming with energy, like an engine with its idle set too high. He pulls a chair out and settles down into it, cupping a wide cup of *café au lait* in his mitt.

"I don't know how you do it, Renault. Even with Jenny here working the tables you were going nonstop for the last five hours."

"Yes," he says, sighing heavily. "It can get pretty crazy here. I appreciate you sharing her with me."

"Me? What? Shar –" I stammer, caught off guard.

Renault laughs heartily, and gives me a knowing look. "Really, my friend? Just how clever do you think you are? A blind man could see what's going on. You two can't keep your eyes off each other for even five minutes. I figured it out before you'd finished your first cup of coffee."

"That's not really very good evidence, Renault. There hasn't been a man in this café yet who could keep his eyes off her."

"Yes, but there's only one that she's looked back at. I'm sorry, my friend, but you are, as you Americans say, busted."

Jenny comes over to us and stands behind Renault's chair, leaning forward and putting her hands on his shoulders.

"You be nice to this one, Renault. He's one of the good guys."

"He'd better be," says the little Frenchman, and looking meaningfully up at me he adds, "It's no trouble at all to slip some powered glass into your coffee, you know. All she has to do is say the word."

"Hey, with your coffee, anything would be an improvement," I say, chuckling at my own joke.

Renault looks hurt and Jenny leans down and kisses the top of his head. "Pay him no mind, Renault. If it's not half scotch he thinks it's just dishwater."

"All the same," says the little man, standing up slowly and moving back toward the kitchen, "I think it might be better if you keep making the coffee, Jenny. I've had some… comments… in the last week."

Jenny giggles loudly and comes over to me and squeezes onto my lap. She brings her lips close to my ear and whispers, "You'd better get out of here before the lunch crowd comes in and you blow our cover with the rest of the town. I'll be home by three. Be sure you're waiting for me, babe. I'm nowhere near finished with you. I figure as long as you can still walk without support, I haven't done my job properly."

By time I slip back into the blazing sunlight and suffocating heat, Jenny and Renault are both in the kitchen, joking with Manuel and loading the big dishwasher with the morning's dishes. On the way to my car an assassin bug whizzes through the air inches from my face, causing me to jerk back and slip and fall on my butt in the gravel. I come down hard, catching myself with my hands, scraping them up on the rough stones and sending a cloud of dust up around me. But as I sit there in the dirt, covered in dust, looking at my bleeding hands, I still can't keep from chuckling contentedly. It looks like it's going to be a beautiful day.

*   *   *

Before long Jenny and I settle into a routine, with her getting up at 4am and groggily dragging herself off to the *Early Riser* while I show up at seven for breakfast. We try our best to act in public like we're just good friends, but sometimes I get the impression some of my fellow diners have twigged to the hidden depths of our relationship. She hasn't been back to her farmhouse except to pick up some more clothes, and for all intents and purposes lives in my apartment with me. The first time she casually refers to it as "our apartment" I catch my breath and almost have to pinch myself.

Very quickly my life starts to revolve around the
Early Riser. It's where I start my days, eat my lunches,
and spend my afternoons, relaxing with Renault and Jenny
when everyone else has left. And now that Jenny is working
full time at the café, its popularity has tangibly increased.
She makes everyone feel welcome and the diners, especially
the older male ones, always want to engage her in
conversation, stopping her as she sweeps by to tell her a joke
or to offer up a compliment, or even just to catch a flash of
her hundred-watt smile.

*   *   *

I'm nursing a cup of coffee one morning, contentedly
digesting another excellent breakfast, when one of my dining
companions makes a curious comment. He's an old bird,
one of the dirt farmers that lives now mostly on government
subsidies while eking-out a subsistence-level income from
the few bushels of peanuts he can squeeze out of his land.
As far as I can tell, most of his activity these days is comprised
of eating leisurely breakfasts and complaining about the
current gang of crooks in Congress.

But as Jenny passes us, refilling our coffee cups and then
twirling away to her next table, he looks over at her and says
quietly, "Now there's a sad case. Married into a family curse
and didn't discover it till it was too late."

I raise my eyebrows at him and it's all he needs to bend
forward and comment conspiratorially, "You know about
her husband and his family, don't you?"

I don't say anything, and he takes that as his cue to
fill me in on the local history.

"That's a tragic story if I ever heard one. Her husband's parents were both killed one night in a head-on collision. Took everyone by surprise, especially their two boys.

"Billy, the older one, took the farm, mostly because I think someone had to and the younger one, Marty, wanted no part of it. But it wasn't more than six months later that Billy was killed, too, in the exact same way. Smushed into pulp by a drunk driver doing 90 on the wrong side of the road.

"From what I heard of it, Marty wasn't going to come back at all, had it in his mind to just sell the place and move on to greener pastures. He and his new wife were living in El Paso, and none of us here ever expected to see him again. But he needed to keep the place up till it sold and, well, you know how it is, one thing led to another, and the offers weren't exactly streaming in, and before you know it he and Jenny were settled in and looking like they'd be here for the long haul.

"And then – bam! He goes off the road one night and that's all she wrote, brother. Three on a match, you know what I mean?"

"That's a tragic story, all right, but I don't know if I'd call it a 'family curse'."

"Well maybe you wouldn't, but that's not what the boy thought. He was convinced that would be his fate. Figured the writing was on the wall for him, talked about it all the time. I guess maybe a part of him made it come true, just out of sheer pigheadedness. But whatever the reason, it's left poor Jenny stuck on her own out there, sitting on a worthless piece of land that ain't worth squat. Poor girl. She deserves better."

As though she's heard us calling her name, Jenny sweeps back out of the kitchen and comes up to our table.

"Are you two liars done swapping tall tales for the day, or do I have to brew up a new pot of coffee before you'll be satisfied?"

Laughing, we push back our chairs and stand up and stretch, and watch her hustle off to the next table to harass another pair of breakfast stragglers.

Poor Jenny, I think. *She deserves better indeed.*

*   *   *

One day a chartered bus pulls up and disgorges its contents into the café, a swarm of noisy adults chattering excitedly and pointing and snapping pictures.

"What's all this about?" I ask Renault as the human flood swirls past us.

"It's a field trip from the art school in Odessa," he tells me. "These are all their paintings that I've hung in the café, and they've come to see their art on display. For many of them, it's the first time they've ever been exhibited in public."

"And probably the only time," I say, eyeballing one particularly bad imitation of a Monet, with skewed perspectives and colour choices that are just a little off from what they should be.

"Now, now, let's not be too critical. These people all have the souls of true artists, even if they were a little shortchanged in the talent department. We should reward the audacity of spirit that allows them to follow their dreams."

"Couldn't we reward them by giving them back their paintings?"

Renault just grins and punches me in the arm. "You're a true philistine, my friend."

RENAULT

ON THE AFTERNOONS when I drop by the café at closing time, Jenny and I sit with Renault for a while, sipping a selection from his excellent wine collection and trading war stories. Renault has an endless store of anecdotes from his previous restaurant jobs in Paris, ranging from the humourous to the appalling; he seems to have worked at half the restaurants in *la belle ville*, and likes to talk about the American tourists who don't realise they're eating horse until after the meal, when he would casually let slip what "cheval" means, and then stand back to watch their horrified expressions.

It's only rarely that I have a story to top one of Renault's, despite my having lived almost everywhere in the civilised world at some point or another.

Most of the time Jenny sits quietly, listening and flickering her eyes back and forth between me and Renault, laughing or squealing at the best anecdotes, and prodding us for more. She catches us off-guard once, telling us a scandalous story about having sex in the boys' locker room at her high school with one of the football players who thought it would be a good prank to run off with her clothes when they were done, stranding her in enemy territory without so much as a stitch to hide beneath. Her solution was to walk calmly, naked as a jaybird, over to the girls' locker room right through the girls' volleyball practice, where sympathetic friends donated enough clothes for her to make it back to class without missing a beat. She ended up suspended for a week, of course, but became a local hero and as a bonus her offending male partner became *persona non grata* for the rest of the year, unable to scare up a single date, even among the freshmen girls. I am starting to suspect that there's hidden depths to this girl who first came to me like a frightened rabbit, chewing on her lip and wringing her hands. Somehow that image just doesn't square with the person I've come to know.

Eventually our shared confidences lead to more frank discussions about our present circumstances and Jenny takes the opportunity to prod Renault about the events that led him to our town.

"I know, I know," she says, waving her hand dismissively, "I've heard the story about the car that broke down, but don't tell me there's not more to it than that. You had no business driving anywhere near this place, we're so far off the beaten path. What's the real story, Renault? C'mon, you can level with us."

It's not the first time she's asked him, and every time he's demurred, deflecting the question and changing the subject, but finally she catches him during a moment of weakness. That, and the wine, loosens his lips, and reluctantly he begins to tell us his story.

"If you ask most Americans about the Mafia, they'll tell you they all come from Sicily, as though it's Italy's national export. But we have plenty of Mafia in France, too. They're big in the south, in Corsica and Marseilles, and scattered here and there throughout the country in the larger cities, and of course, in Paris. In French we call them *Le Milieu*, what you would probably translate as something like 'The Underworld'.

"In the early 1900's their base was in the center part of Paris, in a district called 'Pigalle', but these days that's gotten too seedy for the fat vegetables, who hang out mostly in Montreuil, a little to the east of Pigalle."

Renault stops talking for a moment as he notices the puzzled look on Jenny's face, and the amused one on mine.

"You don't mean 'fat vegetable', Renault," I say between chuckles. "In English it's 'big cheese'. That's what you meant, right? The head honchos, the godfathers?"

"Oh, right, right. Thank you. Yes – godfathers. In French we call them *les parrains*. Sorry. I was trying to be… shall we say, colloquial."

"That's OK. Continue, please."

"Well, as I was saying, the … head honchos … spend their time mostly in Montreuil, where I had my last restaurant. I wasn't the owner, just the manager. It was a place called *Les frères heureux*, which means 'the happy brothers', and

I suppose just the name alone should have tipped me off – it was a nod to two legendary Mafia godfathers from the thirties, the Zemour brothers, who controlled all the prostitution in Paris and then introduced the drug trade on a huge scale.

"I was so happy to be running the place, though, I ignored the nature of the clientele. They were all refined men and expensive women, and they were very generous with their money. Above the restaurant was a very exclusive five-star hotel and it never seemed to be lacking for guests, who all came downstairs to eat. For a restauranteur like myself, it was a dream come true.

"Of course I had to screw it up."

He stops to sip at his wine, and for a moment Jenny and I are afraid that he's reconsidered his decision to unburden himself. We exchange a worried glance, and I debate whether I should break the spell by saying something, but before I can make a sound he starts talking again.

"There was one special lady who used to come drink at the bar in my place. I'm sure you understand what kind of lady she was. On slow nights she would have a light meal, too, and everything always went on her tab. I hadn't noticed at first, but one day I was scanning the books and I discovered she had built up a tab of several thousand euros. No one had ever thought to ask her to settle up. It was clear she'd had a special 'understanding' with the previous management, and the staff kept their noses out of it. I should have, too.

"After I stumbled over her tab I discreetly sat down with her and suggested she pay up. She virtually laughed in my face. Out of the question, she said. But, if I wished, she would be happy to honour the arrangement she had with the previous manager."

Renault takes another drink and pauses in reflection again, but this time he looks peaceful, the way you would when remembering a particularly delightful time in your life.

"You mustn't judge me, my friends. In those days I was working almost sixteen hours a day. Such a schedule doesn't allow for a man to maintain a… social life. And this woman, she was not merely beautiful, she was a dream wrapped in nylon and silk. When she walked into a room every man would hold his breath for a moment, transfixed by her graceful passage. It seemed as though her feet didn't even touch the floor. She *floated* where other women merely walked.

"She suggested that we go upstairs to the hotel and discuss her tab in private, and that's exactly what we did, every Tuesday afternoon, for almost a full year. I believe she came to enjoy my company, at least as much as anyone in her profession can, and I can't deny that I always enjoyed hers.

"What got us in trouble was her little affinity for danger. I told you we visited the hotel every Tuesday afternoon, but I didn't mention that we never paid for a room. She kept a pass key that she had gotten once from a former manager at the hotel, and whenever we visited, she would discreetly glance at the wall behind the front desk – I think you call them 'key cubbies' – and quickly note which of her favourite rooms were vacant. The hotel wouldn't allow anyone to check in before three o'clock, so as long as we left the room before then, we never had any trouble. The danger in possibly getting caught added a touch of spice to her day, I think. I know it almost gave me a heart attack once or twice, but she would only just laugh."

"My particular undoing came as a result of the special

clientele that the hotel and restaurant attracted, which was, of course, the local Mafia. The Callemin family controlled all the heroin trade in France north of Lyon, and one day their *parrain* – their godfather, I mean – was meeting with the godfather of the ruling Corsican family.

"From what I learned later from the newspapers, the Corsicans were in charge of importing heroin through their base in Marseilles, and they controlled the trade from there to as far north as Lyon. The two families intended to make a pact that would streamline their distribution network throughout France. It was a grand gesture for the Corsican to visit Paris in person, but of course the Callemins couldn't leave well enough alone.

"And as luck would have it, the suite in the hotel where they decided to conduct this secret meeting of critical importance happened to be the very selfsame presidential suite which my *courtisane* had chosen that day for our weekly assignation.

"When we heard voices at the door and a key rattling, she leapt out of bed and grabbed her clothes and just barely managed to get away through a service door at one end of the suite – I remember seeing her naked derriere disappear into a discreet passageway just as the door to the hotel corridor opened – but I was frozen in place and I panicked. Clutching my clothes in my arms, I leapt stark naked into a closet by the bathroom and cowered there as the two groups of gangsters filed into the main room.

"I couldn't make out anything that they said during their meeting. All I could hear were some low voices for a while, then a few louder comments, something that was obviously very angry, then quite clearly *'Salaud!'* and *'Voleur!'* –"

Renault quickly looks over to Jenny and says, "Ah, that would be 'bastard' and 'thief'.

"And then, sounding like a cannon going off, several sharp bangs, eight or nine in quick succession, then after a long pause, several deliberate individual shots.

"I read later that the police figure that the Callemins suddenly decided, for some unknown reason, to pull their guns, and killed all four of the Corsicans right off. But apparently one of them didn't die right away, and he managed to pull his gun and catch the four assailants off-guard, wiping them out before succumbing to his wounds.

"You can imagine my terror, hiding there in the closet during such a massacre. I wasn't so scared, though, not to realise this might be my one and only chance to escape before either more gangsters or the police arrived. I dressed as quickly as I could and – as you like to say – got the hell out of Dodge."

Jenny and I are speechless, sitting slack-jawed and motionless, astounded by the story. Of all the scenarios we had imagined, this one had never even entered into the mix. Renault, in contrast, seems energized by the telling of his tale, as though sharing his terrible secret has finally lifted a crushing weight from off his shoulders.

"Gee… Renault, that's an amazing story…" I say, "But I'm wondering how it led you here. If no one saw you, what's the harm? Couldn't you just go back to work as though nothing had happened? Why run away?"

"Ah, well, I have to be honest with you, my friend. There's one little detail I might have left out…."

Jenny leans forward in her chair. She's not actually biting her nails, but that's all you could say. She's hanging on Renault's every word and holding her breath waiting for the rest of the story.

"You see," continues Renault, a little hesitantly, "When I was on my way out of the suite I didn't run quite so fast enough not to notice something laying on the coffee table in the middle of the slaughtered men.

"It was a briefcase. And it was open. And inside it were neatly stacked dozens of little banded packets of money. One million euros, I counted later. Without thinking about it – and if I had I would have left it there, I know that now – I picked up that briefcase and hustled out of the room with it in my arms."

"You stole money from a Mafia godfather," I say, my voice sounding flat and dull.

"Yes, and don't bother lecturing me about the foolishness of what I did. If we carefully considered all our actions in this life, the world would be a much different place."

"Yes, but *the Mafia*, Renault! Haven't you ever watched any movies?"

"Well, once I did it, it was too late to turn back. And for a while I hoped I might actually get away with it. Everyone was dead. There were no witnesses. My presence there was completely unknown.

"Except everyone *wasn't* dead. The Callemin godfather himself survived, in a coma for two months, and it wasn't long after he woke up that people started disappearing. First, a front desk clerk from the hotel failed to show up for work one day, then a few days later, one of the bellmen, then the concierge. I knew it was only a matter of time before someone recalled something that would lead to me or my lady friend.

"Fortunately, I had spent the intervening months well, taking steps that would enable me to slip out of the country along with all the money. I wasn't about to spend another sleepless night waiting for a creaking stair to announce my demise. I hopped on a plane and flew to Canada, and then took a train into New York. In a roundabout way I made it to Texas, and the rest you know. The story about the car is partly true, except I came here deliberately, traveling the most obscure back roads I could find. This town looked like as good a place as any. And I have to say, it's worked out pretty well. No one will ever find me here."

Jenny finally speaks, and her voice has a strange quality to it, sounding almost hungry. "But why do you stay here, Renault? It's been years now. Why aren't you relaxing on a beach somewhere? Why spend your days slaving away in this café?"

When he replies, he looks almost wistful, and his eyes are terribly sad.

"This is all I want to do in life, Jenny. I was born to run a restaurant. I could never endure sitting on a beach waiting to die. This is my dream.

"And besides," he continues, "The money's mostly all gone, now. I sunk it all into this place, and what little is left I use to subsidise the operations. How do you think I paid for the wine you're drinking? The last time I looked, Châteauneuf-du-Pape wasn't produced locally. And the prices I charge for the food don't even cover the cost of the bare ingredients. You see those Belgian endives over there, the ones we braise in white wine and serve with the roast chicken breasts? They're worth their weight in gold. The price of the entire meal doesn't even cover the cost to ship them in."

"I never did think you managed your money all that well," says Jenny. "Those banquettes you had specially built and shipped in from Atlanta must have cost you a small fortune, and each picture frame on that so-called art you hung in the dining room has to be worth more than all the paintings put together. Not to mention the walk-in refrigerators and the new grill you had installed. You might just as well have bought an empty building instead of buying-out the previous owner."

"Ah, but it was never about making money, Jenny. The joy is in the journey, in the work itself. Almost every day someone will tell me that they've just had the best meal they can ever recall eating. To me, that is worth several briefcases of money."

I can see from her expression that she still doesn't get it, but I understand what Renault is saying. For an artist, to create is to live. And Renault is truly alive, here in this small café, in the middle of nowhere.

*   *   *

Later that night, as we're curled up on my couch watching a movie, Jenny is still thinking about Renault.

"You know, hon," she says, pensively, "I don't know if I buy Renault's answer that all the money is gone. There's no way he sunk almost one and a half million dollars into that little dive. He must have a ton of it still socked away somewhere."

"You don't know that. It might have cost him a pretty penny to smuggle the money into the country – he wouldn't want to risk crossing the border with it. Customs would seize anything over $10,000, and international bank transfers would be out of the question – too traceable, and Homeland Security would be all over him like white on rice. He's probably on the level."

"No, sorry…. I just don't buy it. No one blows their stash and leaves themselves out on a limb like that, especially after risking their life to get it. He's got a nest egg tucked away somewhere, I just know it…."

SEÑOR MENDOZA

I KNEW IT was coming, of course. I should have been ready and waiting, with a good story and an even better exit plan, but with every additional day that passes without him making an appearance I shove it further and further back in my mind, stop asking myself what I am going to do and how I will handle the problem. It's exactly as Jenny once reminded me: the hard questions never get asked when life is good.

The morning he shows up starts much like any other, with an excellent breakfast and pleasant conversation, then a quiet walk back to my apartment through the dusty streets. There are clouds in the sky today, and a long dark line over the horizon behind me in the west. It's not likely that any actual rain will fall, though, so the only effect is a slightly increased humidity in the air and a strange flavour to the incessant wind that pushes against my back.

I catch sight of myself as I stride down the street, a wavy doppelgänger reflected back at me from the darkened store windows that aren't boarded up. I hardly recognise the fellow I see: he seems to have a lilt in his step and the air of *someone who belongs*, something I've never laid claim to before. My life up to now has been a solitary journey, one of a carefree nomadic existence built on long-distance relationships, eschewing the down-and-dirty intimacies of close personal connections. It's no coincidence that all my friends are scattered across the globe, accessible only by email or phone, comfortably and safely at arm's distance. Never threatening, never challenging, never demanding any more of me than what I want to give.

Jenny has changed all that, transformed me as dramatically as any metamorphosis I ever could have imagined. Whether by magic or witchcraft or through simple feminine wiles, she has wiped away every trace of my former lifestyle to where my day doesn't really begin until I'm with her, and where time spent away from her company seems wasted and without purpose. I'm losing myself in her, and the scariest thought of all is that I'm happy about it.

Two crows are standing in the middle of the street ahead of me, pulling at the corpse of some unfortunate beast who made the fatal misjudgment of cutting through town last night, only to meet his fate in the unlikeliest of ways – squashed by probably the only car to pass through town between sundown and sunrise. The crows look up at me intermittently as my path brings me closer to them, then finally squawk complainingly as they flutter up and away over the buildings. *Even the crows travel in pairs*, I think, and smile in quiet satisfaction. *I guess it's high time I got in sync with the rest of the world.*

I open the door to my building and even before my foot hits the first stair I know he's there. And I know immediately that my life is about to change dramatically once again.

It's the smell of cigar smoke that gives him away. I follow the stench up the stairs and through the open doorway into my office. He's sitting in the dark in my chair behind the desk, the glowing red ember on the tip of his cigar floating like a disembodied spirit in front of his face.

He's drinking my Scotch, too, but has left the second glass in the drawer. I guess I'm not invited to the party. I note peripherally that the liquid in the bottle is getting low, and I file a mental note to remind myself to pick up a new bottle the next time I'm out.

"Smoking isn't permitted in here," I say quietly.

"Well, I didn't think you'd mind too much," come the words back at me, floating in a silken, soft voice oozing from a man who never has to raise it to get what he wants. His English sounds almost perfect, but a trace of a Mexican accent still creeps into it. "After all, we can't let ourselves get upset by the little things in life, now can we?" He chuckles softly and I see his arm wave out in an expansive gesture as he indicates the visitor's chair in front of the desk.

"Sit down, my friend. We have much to discuss. Come. Sit, relax."

I sit down, but somehow I don't think I'm going to be doing much relaxing.

"I have to hand it to you," he says, pausing briefly to inhale some poison from the little death stick in his hand. "That was a very smooth operation you pulled out in the desert."

If he's waiting for a reaction from me, I don't give him any. I can feel his eyes studying me in the dark, and I sit motionless in my chair, waiting to see how this will play out.

"I was quite puzzled, at first," he continues. "I made the connection immediately, of course, when that pathetic creature was arrested in Odessa with a truck full of my product. But that's only where the confusion began.

"First, it was an elegant little performance, far too slick for that hick to have managed. Not to mention that he would never have had the *cojones* to rip me off. And when I watched the surveillance video of inside the lab, the confident figure in a wrestler's hood that moved about in the hut displayed a precise conservation of movement. Efficient. Disciplined. Completely out of character for the twitchy little fellow found holding my stock."

Another pause, another brief burst of glowing ember, another quiet stream of exhaled smoke, and then he resumes talking.

"I just needed to talk with him for a few minutes, but the DA in Odessa decided to take a special interest in our little friend, and circumstances prevented me or my associates from obtaining any private time with him. Until recently, that is. Once he was moved into general holding we were able to sit down and have a really productive conversation.

"It was quite a fascinating story he told us, about a fellow from the St. Louis Mob who told him that this county – *my* county – was in fact their territory. Again, when I heard this my confusion only deepened. If anyone from St. Louis were in my area, surely I would have known about it. It had to be someone local working for them.

"That was a nice touch, though. Using a Missouri license plate. No doubt you made quite sure the little loser got a good look at it. It sent me down the wrong path, too, and I wasted valuable time making a lot of fruitless inquiries.

"But I kept coming back to a local connection, and inevitably you showed up on my radar. And when I found this in the trunk of your car –" he reaches down and pulls up something that he tosses onto the desk in front of me. It is the wrestler's hood. It must have slipped down underneath my spare tire in the floor of the trunk and been laying there ever since; I had completely forgotten about it. "That's when everything clicked.

"Don't beat yourself up over it, my friend. It's an understandable error, and the devil, as we say, is in the details. There's almost always some little thing that even the best of us overlook.

"I found it about a week ago and I've been mulling over how I wanted to handle this situation. You might be a very handy addition to my local talent, and you obviously weren't going anywhere, so I decided to sit back and study you for a while.

"And I'm so glad I didn't move too quickly. Imagine my delight when I was woken up at 5am this morning by the clerk from the motel east of town, telling me about two very serious gentlemen driving a vehicle with Missouri plates, who checked-in just before dawn.

"This surprise development should help clear away many nagging little details, such as how you were going to replace the money you stole from me. It's hardly a meaningful sum, just a few days' revenue, but the principle of the thing prevents me from overlooking it – that would send the wrong message to so many people.

"The product I really don't care about. The proverbial drop in the ocean, don't you know. We barely skipped a beat replacing that lab's production. It's annoying to lose the site, but there's a lot of land out here. It's not like we can't find another bare patch of ground to set up another hut.

"But your friends from St. Louis who have come to check up on you have many resources at their disposal. I'm sure we can find a way to persuade them to reimburse me for their ill-advised foray into my business, and in the process send an unmistakable message that this area is *not* up for grabs. I don't relish the thought of tangling with the Mafia, but I won't shrink from doing so, either."

It would be an understatement to say that my mind was awash in a maelstrom of thoughts. If matters weren't already bad enough, now I had an additional vector of hostility to negotiate. Things were starting to unravel quicker than I could keep up. I might have been able to find a way to stay alive when dealing with only this particular gentleman, but the Mob takes a very dim view of people impersonating them. Any life insurance actuary worth his salt would no doubt shake his head and tsk-tsk very discouragingly at the effect this most recent news would have on his calculations of my life expectancy.

"I think this would be an excellent time to go pay a visit on your friends," says my visitor, standing up and dropping the stub of his cigar into the glass. "I suspect their late arrival has delayed their morning schedule, so if we hurry we might be able to catch them before they leave for the day. Shall we?" And he motions toward the door, which is still standing open, just as I had found it.

I've been around long enough to know when to make my move, and when to hang back and wait for the right opportunity. I'm not anxious to go anywhere with this individual, but there's still too much about him I don't know yet.

As he moves closer to the light I get my first good look at him. He's not a tall man, but he's not small and wiry like Renault, either. I've seen his type exercising in the gym, men of lesser height who compensate for their diminished stature by developing rock-hard bodies, lean and perfectly toned. I have no doubt that beneath his suit there is nothing but muscle, and he moves with a smooth graceful motion that hints at a boxer's training. I'm not certain he would even need a weapon to kill me. And since I'm unarmed, that doesn't leave me with a lot of options.

"Do you have a name," I say, "Or should I just stick with 'Hey you'?"

He chuckles good-naturedly and grins. "You may call me 'Mendoza', if you wish, or 'Señor Mendoza' if you're feeling especially subservient," and he chuckles again.

He lets me precede him down the stairs and once we're on the street he walks me round the corner to where he's parked his SUV out of sight of my building's entrance. It's big and black, with impenetrably-dark tinted windows, a rolling cliché. I suppose he kept it out of sight so as not to telegraph his presence, probably more out of force of habit than out of concern that I might derive an advantage from any foreknowledge of his arrival. Maybe he just didn't want to scare me away and have to track me down again.

I suppose he's talked all he feels he needs to, and we drive east in silence. I look downwards through my window at the road zipping away beside us. The blur of its passage seems to mirror my own thoughts, smeared and indistinct, unable to focus or figure out a way to salvage any satisfactory resolution to this mess I'm in. An assassin bug crawls carefully along the glass just above the door frame, holding on tightly to keep from being blown off. I wonder where he thinks he's going, and why he doesn't leap off and fly away to safety. I know I would if I were him.

THe WISEGUYS

IT'S NOT a long trip, and suddenly we're slowing down as we come up on the seedy 4-unit motel whose neon VACANCY sign hasn't been turned off in all the time I've been living here. The entire motel consists of one long, squat building, stucco walls painted white about two decades ago and that's obviously still good enough for the current Management. There's not much else to it, aside from four large windows evenly spaced out across the expanse of stucco, each paired with one of four identical doors with peeling blue paint and sporting hardware store decals identifying them as 1, 2, 3, or 4. A door at the end of the building closest to the highway is marked *Office*, and the top half of it is a glass window, with a little venetian blind hanging partly lowered, in exactly the same position it has been in since the day I first stayed here years ago.

We pull into the lot and park beside an identical big, black SUV sitting directly in front of Unit 1. Heavy curtains are pulled across the room's window, and a little plastic card hangs from the door handle sporting the message: *Do Not Disturb*. There are no other vehicles in the lot, and no signs whatsoever of any human presence at any of the other rooms. I guess we won't be needing to ask the clerk for directions to the room we want.

No explanations or instructions are needed. We both get out and walk up to the door with the "1" on it, and he nods at me. The inference is clear.

I don't have a lot of room here for improvisation. There's nothing to do but knock, so I make a fist and pound heavily on the door.

The place was silent before I banged, and it stays silent, but now the silence has a different feel to it. It almost screams of suspicious glances exchanged on the other side of the door, of cautious, furtive movements and noiseless hand signals. Nothing happens, so after about twenty seconds I bang again.

This time, there's a response.

"What is it?" comes short and quick from behind the wall, in a voice that's pulled off to the side, wary, unwelcoming.

"Hey guys," I say, wracking my brain for a phrase that will produce an acceptable response. "Open the door. It's me."

"Fuck off." The response is short and to the point.

"Hey," I say, sounding peeved, "Quit screwing around, you two. Lemme in. It's hot as fuck out here. I'm in no mood."

I almost leap back in surprise as the door is yanked open, explosively and without warning. The man in the room is big – not muscular, just fat. The good life has been just a little too good for him, and the pounds hang heavily on his flesh. He doesn't need to be in very good shape, though, because the gun in his left hand looks like it's been doing all the heavy lifting for him for the last few years. He's wearing a rumpled suit with a dark jacket over a white shirt that needs to be washed. He's not wearing a tie, or any shoes over his black silk socks, and he looks like he could do with another couple hours' sleep.

I grit my teeth and decide to go for the gold.

"Holy shit, you took your time," I say, stepping forward and pushing past him into the room. He stares at me goggle-eyed and instinctively steps back as I stride past him. His sleep-addled brain hasn't come to terms yet with this strange turn of events, and the confusion is writ large on his face. "Hope you don't mind, I brought some company with me." And I gesture dismissively over my shoulder at the man behind me on the sidewalk.

This little bit of added information seems to do it for him, snapping him out of his funk and into reality. I may have caught him off-guard, but Mendoza virtually screams of imminent threat, a serious, dangerous individual that sets the alarm bells ringing wildly in the big man's brain. His first reaction, of course, is to raise his gun and to swing it in the little man's direction.

"What the f –" is as far as he gets before Mendoza's hand moves as well, so fast it's almost a blur, disappearing into his suit jacket and reemerging instantaneously with a large automatic pistol in its grip, firing two quick shots that impact first in the big man's throat, and then in his forehead.

There's another man in the room, dressed almost identically to his now-deceased roommate, and when his buddy staggers back and tumbles into the room he makes a tentative motion with his gun, but he can't make up his mind where to point it, as his first impulse to draw a bead on me is conflicted by this new revelation of an actual threat holding an actual gun. I had briefly held first place in his attention by virtue of my initial entrance into the room, but both my hands are unmistakably weapon-free, unlike those of Intruder #2, who may have arrived late to the party, but who definitely now commands the full attention of everyone still standing.

The man in the room makes his choice and swivels the gun over towards my erstwhile companion but freezes in mid-motion at the sight of the pistol pointed unmistakably at his face.

"Uh-uh," says the little Mexican. "Don't be stupid."

It's good advice, and the man in the room takes it. Slowly, he drops to one knee and carefully lowers his gun and places it on the floor, then even more slowly raises both his hands up shoulder-high.

Mendoza steps fully into the room, never taking his eyes off his target, and swings the door shut behind him.

"What the fuck is all this?" asks the other man, still on one knee. "You have any idea who we are? You're a dead man, buddy."

"Shut up. I'm not here to make new friends. I'm going to ask you one question only, and you have one chance to give me the answer I want.'

"You're a dead man."

"Yes, I believe you already made that point. However, at the moment I'm the one holding the gun, and you're the one on his knees. Now listen carefully: as you know, your friend over here has deprived me of a significant amount of product and cash, and reparations need to be made. Do you have the authority to make such an appeasement, or can you contact someone who can?"

"You're a fucking lunatic, buddy. You have no fucking clue what you're doing. You're a dead ma—"

The man on the floor has no chance to finish his thought, as the little Mexican lifts his gun and sends two slugs into his forehead. He sighs heavily and wipes off the barrel of his pistol by lifting up the newly-deceased man's sleeve and using it as a rag.

"That conversation was getting boring. A pity some people just can't think outside the box."

He slides his pistol back under his suit jacket and looks at me with a tired expression.

"Well, we tried it the easy way, but now I'm afraid we'll have to change our strategy. I'm giving you 72 hours to contact your people in St. Louis and have them deliver into your hands every single penny of what you took from me. I will come by your place and pick it up three days from now at exactly –" he glances at his wristwatch – "11:42 am.

"Now, you're a clever guy and I'm sure I don't have to tell you this, but don't even bother wasting your time thinking about running. Regardless whether you head north or east, you wouldn't make it fifty miles before one of my friends caught up to you. I suppose you could try heading south or west, of course, but I'm not certain that would work out any better. Strange things happen to gringos in Mexico, especially gringos who piss in the wrong places and make all the wrong enemies. No, I'm afraid your best course of action rests with convincing your friends in St. Louis that they need to cover your ass on this one.

"And then once we're clear of that little debt, you and I can sit down and have a serious discussion about your future career path. As I said, I'm always looking for capable personnel. This just might turn out to be your lucky break."

He turns and steps over the dead body laying behind him, then opens the door and moves into the sunlight, pulling it shut and leaving me alone in the room with the two corpses.

My head is swimming. I almost feel the need to pat down my body checking for holes. I quickly frisk each of the two dead men and pull out their wallets. They both have long multisyllabic Italian-sounding names and St. Louis addresses on their driver's licenses. The fat guy doesn't look like me in the slightest, but the driver's license in the other guy's wallet has a pretty blurry photo taken four years earlier, and might pass for an earlier version of me. I pocket his wallet and then notice a significant bulge in the fat man's pants pocket. I reach in and pull out a thick folded wad of cash. Apparently, credit cards are not the preferred method of payment for the discerning wiseguy of today.

On the bureau is a set of car keys and a fob, along with a little metal tag embossed with the Italian flag. I want to search their car, but I can't risk being seen poking around in a vehicle belonging to two newly-minted corpses.

The sound of the shots almost certainly made it to the motel office, but I'm not worried about the desk clerk calling the police anytime soon. Even if he wasn't sleeping in the back room, he's probably too smart to go alerting the authorities without waiting long enough to let the Mexican make his departure. There's simply no percentage in it for him to be a good citizen and to start ringing alarm bells. Much better that the maid find the bodies later in the day. If there even is a maid, that is.

I grab a hand towel from the bathroom and use it to turn the doorknob and open the door. I do the same in reverse on the outer handle, then drop the towel on the sidewalk. Five minutes later I'm well away from the motel, hoofing it rapidly down the road, alert for any oncoming vehicles, which thankfully are nonexistent.

I'm still fifteen minutes away from my place when I feel the impact of several fat raindrops. I guess I was wrong about the chances for rain today. They patter down unenthusiastically on the pavement around me, sending up a thick, musty aroma of disturbed dust and ozone. Little droplets of oil appear on the asphalt, making the road look like it's bleeding from a million tiny pinpricks. Within minutes, however, the imitation shower ends, petering away as quietly as it began, leaving the air thick with humidity.

STORM clouds

THE WALLET in my pocket burns away at me until I'm back at my place. It's an irrefutable, death-sentence connection with the two dead men at the motel, and I can't think of any explanation I could possibly invent that would justify its presence without sending me to the slammer.

The wad of greenbacks is a different matter. But despite the glorious anonymity of cash it still bothers me to carry it around, with some irrational, paranoid sector of my brain screaming that it's an incriminating link to the carnage in the motel.

So before I go upstairs to my apartment, I detour to the rear lot and pop the trunk on my car. There's a thick felt covering along the bottom and sides of the trunk, and I reach in and grip the flap that runs up the right side. I pull it back from the metal and wedge the cash beneath it as far as I can, then do the same with the wallet. That will do for the immediate short-term, but I'm determined to find a better place for the wallet at the earliest opportunity.

When I get upstairs my distress only seems to intensify. Frantically, I pace back and forth, trying to sort out the best course of action to follow. I never bothered counting to see how much money was in that bin, but I used up five bricks to frame Willie, and judging by their thickness, I'm assuming that translates to $125,000. It might as well be a million. Mendoza was pretty clear about wanting the whole sum.

And when Mendoza comes back here in three da—.

I freeze in my tracks at the thought.

Jenny!

I can't have Jenny showing up on Mendoza's radar – it's possible he hasn't linked the two of us yet. We're still being very discreet, and out of pure coincidence she's been splitting her time during the last week between the café and her farmhouse, taking care of some necessary housekeeping matters, hiring a yard crew to keep the weeds at bay, and talking to a couple of local ranchers about leasing out her land to grow winter wheat; ironically, letting the ground lay fallow for the last couple years and not tilling it may have actually been the best course to follow.

But she was going to head over here this afternoon after work, and I need to prevent that from happening. I check my watch – it's just a few minutes after 2. It took me longer to walk back from the motel than I had expected. Distances seem so much shorter when we move across them at 60 miles an hour; the ten-minute drive to the motel took me almost two hours to walk back.

I've formed a rough plan of action in my mind and I start in on it by driving to the café. When I turn into the lot I'm puzzled to see only a couple of spots filled, and when I notice that one of the two vehicles is a big, black SUV with dark tinted windows, my blood runs cold. Before I have a complete stroke, however, I notice it has Texas license plates, and I breathe a little easier. As I walk by it on my way to the café's entrance, I discreetly glance at the windshield, where a little monthly parking pass decal from a garage in Houston is affixed. Which means it's not a rental, and therefore not being driven by an out-of-state visitor. I reflect that my paranoia's running in high gear, and I deliberately take a deep breath to force myself to calm down and to clear my thoughts.

Jenny meets me as soon as I step inside the door and her eyes have a strange alertness to them, a puzzling combination of anticipation and apprehension that leaves me wondering if she's scared, worried, or excited.

"Hey babe," she says to me in a hushed tone, "Renault is closing up the café early today. A couple of guys have come to see him about some renovations, and he gave me and Manuel our paychecks in advance for the next week's work. As soon as Chester finishes eating that piece of pie we're done for the day. I'll be over at our place in about twenty minutes."

"Um, no, that won't work. Something has come up, a little problem with an old client, and I need to take care of it. Don't come over until I call you. If I can, I'll come by the farmhouse tonight, but you need to keep away from my place."

Her eyes switch now to full worry-mode, and she says, "What is it? Is something wrong? Are you in danger?"

"No no no," I lie. "Just an unpleasant chore that I need to handle, but I want you to stay out of the way. You've got enough on your plate. In fact, why don't you go visit your sister in El Paso for a few days? You've got the time off, and you deserve a break. I'll call you when my business here is done – I might even come up and join you. Everything's fine, don't worry."

I can tell she doesn't believe me but she's smart enough to know that she won't get anywhere with badgering me right now; that's something she can work on the next time she sees me. Reluctantly, she gives me a quick peck on the cheek and I slip back out to the parking lot, and just before I drive away I see her locking the door behind Chester, who shuffles out looking peeved, unhappy not to be able to linger over his customary post-pie coffee in his usual booth.

I turn west and head toward the sulky horizon, which is now an uncharacteristically mottled dark grey flecked with sporadic flashes of lightning. Again, a few thick raindrops splatter on my windshield, but peter out even before I need to turn on the wipers. I reflect that this is probably the most ideal form of precipitation that this area could hope for, falling sparingly and intermittently, giving the ground a chance to absorb the moisture instead of rolling away in a torrent. Red won't need to go corpse-hunting tomorrow.

When I get to the surface road I'm looking for I turn south and follow it all the way down to I-20, and then turn east. I want to make a wide loop on my way to my shed. It will give me an opportunity to study the cars around me to see if I'm being followed.

I'm not, though. When I turn back north on my way to the shed there's not another vehicle anywhere in sight as far as the eye can see. I breathe a tiny sigh of relief and drive a little more calmly until I hit the dirt road turnoff, then bounce on down to the little hut. When I arrive I grab a duffel bag from the back seat and head directly over to the rusty oil drum behind the shed.

I stick my hand in to grab a couple bricks of cash and immediately regret it, as it appears I've disturbed a nest of assassin bugs who have colonized the drum as their new home. A thick swarm of them explodes up out of the drum around my face, causing me to stagger back, waving frantically in the air. The hand I stuck down into the drum is leaping in pain and I see two huge welts on it where a pair of the nasty little creatures impaled me, injecting their toxic venom deep into my flesh.

Cursing, I gingerly step back to the drum and cautiously peer down over the lip. It appears to be devoid of any other uninvited guests but I'm not taking any chances, and instead of reaching back down into it I push it over on its side and let the contents tumble out onto the ground.

Another bad idea. One of the jugs of benzene topples out along with the money and its cap comes loose, spilling a stream of clear liquid all over several of the shrink-wrapped bricks of money. Quickly, I grab the bricks one by one and lift them away from the liquid and shake them off, as I'm pretty certain the benzene will dissolve the plastic. That would really be the icing on the cake – *"Sorry, Señor Mendoza, but I poured a toxic solvent onto your money and it's all been dissolved into mush."* I'm sure that would go over *real* well.

I grab the bottle of benzene and reattach the cap, then lean over to continue picking up the spilled bricks of money, and suddenly I can't stop leaning over, and I fall forward onto my face, where I notice the ground seems to be swirling around me in a twisting orbit. It takes me over a minute to regain my senses before I can stand up again. Shaking the ants and thorns off my collar and scraping the dirt off my face, I make a mental note not to breathe deeply while leaning over puddles of benzene. I'm sure learning lots of lessons today.

Finally, I finish gathering up the bricks of cash and stuffing them into the duffel. I stand the oil drum up again and carefully replace the half-empty bottle of benzene, then move over to my car and pop the trunk.

I chuckle to think that this morning I was nervous about walking around with just a few thousand dollars in cash in my pocket. I can't begin to imagine what I could say to explain a duffel bag with a few *hundred* thousand dollars in it. *"It's my retirement savings"*?

Before I close up the trunk I pull up the felt cover again and grab the wallet. There's a little interior pocket in the duffel bag that would probably escape a casual inspection, but any thorough examination by a serious individual – a state trooper or DEA agent, for example – would spot it immediately. I shove the wallet into the little pocket and zip it up. I'm not sure how this might play out, or even if it ever will, but it could eventually be an elegant way to tie whoever takes the bag from me to a double homicide. It wouldn't be clear that I'm the one who put it there, so I might not be a target of any angry revenge. And in the meantime, the bag holder would have much more pressing matters on his agenda

than little ol' me. It's a slim hope, but it's an opportunity
not to be overlooked.

It starts raining on me again so I hurry up and shove the
duffel bag deep into the trunk then hop into the driver's seat
and pull back onto the dirt track. It's coming down steadily
enough now that my car doesn't kick up any dust as I bounce
back to the main road. By time I turn onto it, though,
the rain has stopped again. Just what this county needs:
a bipolar weather system.

*   *   *

It's getting close to 4pm when I get back and as I approach
town I slow down a bit when I come up on the motel.
I expected to see police tape, maybe the coroner's van,
or at least the sheriff's cruiser sitting in the parking lot.
Instead, there's nothing at all. Even the black SUV is gone.
It looks as quiet and deserted as a school parking lot on
a Sunday afternoon. Evidently, Management has decided
to pursue a solution that doesn't involve alerting the local
constabulary.

Fortunately, that's none of my business, and I am far more
concerned about what's going on at the *Early Riser*. Jenny's
story about Renault closing for "renovations" – suddenly, in
the middle of the day, with mysterious out-of-town visitors –
doesn't sound even remotely kosher to me. I decide to make
a quick stop at the café and make sure the little Frenchman
is OK.

When I pull up at the café, the first thing I notice is the
big front window, which has been covered from the inside
with sheets of newspaper, completely obscuring any view of
the dining room. The door is papered-over, too, and when

I knock, there's no response. A hand-written sign taped to the inside of the glass door says: "Temporarily closed for renovations", but it's not in Renault's or Jenny's handwriting.

I get back in my car and drive around to the back, and find parked behind the café the black SUV with the Texas plates. I park beside it and walk up and bang heavily on the metal door at the rear of the building that leads into the kitchen.

No response.

I bang again. Still no response.

Jenny showed me once where Renault keeps a couple of emergency keys tucked away inside a weatherproof electrical box near the door. I grab one then unlock the café's door, pull it open and step inside the dark kitchen, letting the door swing shut behind me.

My eyes need a moment to adjust to the dimly-lit deserted restaurant. I can see through the large cutout between the kitchen and the dining room; the outside light is shining against the sheets of newspaper taped over the big window, illuminating the dining room with a soft indirect glow that partially filters into the kitchen. The place is dead quiet, without even so much as a dripping faucet or the hum of the air conditioner to fill the silence.

Until, that is, I hear a single, sharp, metallic click behind my right ear.

"Not a move, now, sweetheart. Not a single fucking move," says a hard voice behind me.

I can't tell you what happens next, although my mind wants to believe I see sunbursts and little starry explosions. But I think it's more accurate to say that everything suddenly just goes black.

TRiPLE THREAT

HEN I WAKE UP my head is throbbing about as much as you'd think it would, and instinctively I lift my hand to my head to see if my hair is matted with blood. At least, that what I try to do, and I'm momentarily confused why I'm having trouble performing such a simple act, until I realise that my hands are wrapped up tightly in front of me and tied to my belt with duct tape.

I'm sitting partially upright, propped against a wall in the dining room, beside the doorway leading into the kitchen. Renault is sitting beside me, tied in a similar manner, but he looks even worse than I do. At least, I hope he looks worse than I do – I'd hate to think I look that bad. His face is dripping with blood and both his eyelids are puffed up to the size of small apricots. His lips are cut and swollen, and his jaw doesn't quite look right, as though it's not properly aligned.

He's also missing an ear. The spot on his head where it used to be is just a bloody hole covered with matted strands of hair.

"Sleeping Beauty's awake," says a voice from behind the dining counter.

The voice is attached to a large man in his early forties wearing a dark suit, and he moves out from around the counter and comes toward me.

His suit is expensive but fits unevenly, a little too big in the shoulders and too tight around the waist. His pants have a small stain on the right thigh, and his shoes are scuffed.

And he's ugly. His eyes are small and beady and too close together. His nose is crooked and looks like it was badly set every time it's been broken, which appears to be several times, at least. There's a tiny nick in his left ear, and a piece missing from his left eyebrow, where a thin scar runs up his forehead and disappears beneath his hairline. He needs a shave, and his five-o'clock shadow looks mangy and uneven. Behind it, his face is greasy and pock-marked, and his teeth are crooked. Several of them are different shades, which would indicate caps over missing molars. He looks like God was working on building a junkyard dog, and then at the last minute was called away and one of his assistants finished the job and made it human.

He comes right up to where I'm sitting on the floor and squats down on his haunches in front of me.

"You're gonna die," he says, staring directly into my eyes.

As introductory lines go, it certainly does the trick of catching my attention. But if he's saying it as a negotiating tactic, in my opinion his strategy leaves a lot to be desired.

"And I'm the one who's gonna kill you. With this gun, right here," he adds, reaching underneath his suit jacket with his right hand and extracting a slim automatic pistol.

Once I've gotten a good chance to admire his hardware, he slips it back into place underneath his suit jacket and brings his hand back out to where I can see it dangling casually in front of my face as he props his elbows on his thighs. The knuckles are swollen and there are dark red smudges on several places on his hand. I can see what appears to be black dirt underneath his nails. Looking closer, the dirt under his fingernails looks like it might be dried blood.

"So you've got nothing to gain from keeping your mouth shut. One way or another, you're leaving this building feet first. But it's up to you how your final minutes are spent – you can choose writhing in agony or peaceful relaxation. It all depends how you answer my questions.

"All clear?"

"Is that one of the questions?" I croak.

His answer is an immediate demonstration for me of how he got all those messy red stains on his right hand, as his fist rockets straight out and into my left eyeball, smashing my head back against the wall and sending starbursts shooting into my brain.

"Now, I'm gettin' the impression," he says after a moment, massaging his fist with his other hand, "That you're a wise-ass. And in my experience, wise-asses never pick the 'peaceful relaxation' option. Which is a pity, I think. Tell me, buddy, are you a wise-ass?"

"Again, I'd really like to know if that's one of the ques–"

This time, it's my right eye that gets it, and the starbursts have turned into an honest-to-goodness fireworks extravaganza in my brain.

"What the hell's going on in there?" comes a second voice from the kitchen, followed by the sound of footsteps indicating the entrance of another player into the scene. I can't see too clearly anymore, but by squinting I can make out the mottled image of another dark-suited individual, who walks over to me and bends over, peering at my face.

"Holy crap, Leon, go easy on him. We don't wanna kill him before Ice Pick has all the information he needs. The other little shit is a write-off. This guy might be our last chance."

"Relax, I'm not killing anyone. I'm just warming him up, is all. Explaining the rules to him, right? That way, when Ice Pick gets here, he'll be more cooperative."

"Yeah, well I've seen the way you explain the ru— shit, now what?"

The sudden banging sounds that explode from the back door thunder through the café like a cannon volley. They are immediately followed by a rough, impatient voice that calls out, "Leon! Tommy! Open up! Move your ass!"

The one called Tommy spins and runs over to the back door and yanks it open like it's on fire.

There's an indistinct silhouette on the other side, and I can't quite figure out its shape until it draws closer and I see it's not just one body, but two. A third big man wearing a dark suit walks into the dining room carrying a duffel bag, and pushing along in front of him at gunpoint a smaller man who stumbles forward into the middle of the room. That man is Señor Mendoza.

"Look what I found in the parking lot searching this other asshole's car," says the big man.

"And look what I saw him take out of the trunk." And he tosses the duffel bag onto the lunch counter.

Leon walks over to the counter and looks into the duffel bag and purses his lips in a silent whistle. "Shit, boss, how much is in here, do you think?"

"I haven't had a chance to look closely, but judging from the weight, there's probably close to a million. Maybe more."

"That's my money," says Mendoza, quietly.

Al three men start laughing loudly, and Leon extends his arm straight out and points the gun in his hand directly at Mendoza. Walking up to him, he presses the tip of the barrel into the very center of his forehead and says, "Say that again."

Mendoza doesn't move a muscle and stands perfectly silent, until Leon steps back and lowers his weapon very slightly and says, "Yeah. That's what I thought."

He turns his head back toward his buddies standing behind him at the lunch counter and, smirking, says, "These fuckin' greasers shut up good when they've go—"

He shouldn't have turned his head. Mendoza moves so fast he's almost a blur as he steps forward, grabs the pistol, and twists the hand holding it upwards and back. Clearly audible, even over the tremendous shriek of pain that comes from Leon, is the sound of several small bones snapping as his wrist rotates around and backwards at a sickening angle. As Mendoza moves to yank the pistol out of Leon's limp fist, the sound of a gun firing explodes in the room, and a huge bloody gash appears in the side of Mendoza's head, accompanied by a small shower of skull fragments and blood that spray out into the air behind him.

The big guy who had walked Mendoza into the room is still holding his gun level, ready to fire again, but there's no need, as the little Mexican slowly crumples to the ground and lays there motionless.

"The little asshole broke my wrist!" screams Leon, cradling his hand in his other palm. "I'm gonna tear hi–"

"You're going to do nothing," says the boss man, walking over to Mendoza's body and giving it a sharp kick in the groin. The body on the floor twitches then resumes its motionless pose. "Good. He's not dead. I got questions for him. Tommy, you drag him over there with those other two. Tie him good, too. We don't want any more injuries, you got that?

"And you, you idiot – pick up your damned gun. How friggin' stupid can you be, you moron. Turning your back on him like that. You're lucky he didn't blow your damn head off. Go find some bandages or towels in the kitchen and wrap that hand up. And now we have to find a sawbones somewhere in this piece-of-shit desert to fix you up. Just. Fucking. Great."

Tommy drags Mendoza over to the wall to my right and props him against it, then proceeds to tape his wrists together and to tie them to his belt. The bleeding from the wound on his head is still trickling down onto his neck but it seems to be subsiding fairly quickly, and he's quietly moaning as he starts to regain consciousness. It looks like the bullet may have grazed him pretty deeply, but missed causing any fatal damage.

Tommy finally finishes tying up Mendoza and straightens up to admire his handiwork while his boss upends the duffel bag onto the lunch counter and pours out the stacks of cash.

"Tommy, when you're finished practicing for your Boy Scout knot-tying badge, come over here and count this."

"Sure thing, boss. Nothin' I like better than countin' money."

The big man moves away from the counter to give
Tommy room to work, and as he steps closer to the front
window I get a better look at him in the light seeping through
the newspapers.

He's just as big a man as Leon, but there's a hardness to
him that Leon lacks. He walks with an easy gait, but there's
no wasted movement, as though he's intent on conserving his
energy for more important tasks. The suit looks expensive
and, judging from the way it fits his physique, is custom-
tailored. His trousers have a crease on them sharp enough
to slice bread, and his shoes are new, highly polished and
perfectly spotless, as though they've never been walked in
outside. He is clean-shaven and his haircut looks like it was
expensive, and the nails on his hands are clean and manicured.

Almost as though he's just remembered about an
important task he needs to attend to, he suddenly turns
his head and looks at me. He comes over and squats down
on his haunches in front of me just as Leon had earlier.
I hope this interview goes a little better than that one did.

"Now, we haven't been properly introduced," he says, still
holding his gun and waving it back and forth in a tight little
pattern while he rests his forearm on his thigh. "My mother
calls me 'Anthony', but the other people I know call me
'Ice Pick'. Now why do you think they call me that?"

"Is it because your dick is the width of a drinking straw?"
I ask, and immediately regret it. I really need to learn to keep
my mouth shut sometimes.

The man is so dumbfounded to be insulted by someone in
my position that he doesn't immediately know how to react.
He obviously had something clever in mind that he was going
to use to follow up his rhetorical question, but now the words

catch in his mouth and trip him up, preventing him from doing much more than gurgling incoherently. It's not long, though, before he regains his composure.

"Oh, so you're a funny guy. Well, that's OK. I like funny guys. We get along. I like a good joke as much as the next guy. Hey – wanna hear another joke?" and he reaches down to my left hand that's tied to my belt, and grabs the little finger and the ring finger, and quickly pushes them backwards until they are both pressed against the back of my hand.

If he was hoping to hear me scream, he gets his wish. I let loose a yowl that surprises even me with its volume. The intense pain subsides pretty quickly, though, and I have to assume that there are already so many endorphins flooding my brain stem that there's not much left for me to feel but short little jolts.

Ice Pick lets go of my fingers and they flop uselessly forward. Normally, I would have thought that moving them like that would actually pop them right off my hand, but thankfully they stay attached.

"How did you like that," he says, grinning maliciously. "Pretty funny joke, eh?"

"Almost as good…" I croak, "As the one about your mother and my di–"

This time he's not caught off-guard, and he doesn't bother with finesse. He backhands me in the mouth with his pistol and I watch, almost from a distance, it seems, as two of my teeth spray out of my mouth and onto the floor to my left.

"I can do this all day," he says, in a hard tone that indicates to me that there's no way he has the patience to do this all day. "You want me to start cutting pieces off you? You want me to go get the power tools? Drill a few extra holes in you?"

I may be pretty dumb, but I'm not completely stupid.
I choose to say nothing, and settle for just glaring at him.
He didn't appreciate the repartee, anyways.

"Now," he says, with a sort of finality that indicates he
believes our preliminary terms of engagement have been
settled, "I'm not interested in you. I only care about that bag
of money that was in your car. Does it belong to this little
shit?" – and, pointing with his gun, with a flick of his wrist
he indicates Renault – "Or this little shit" – and with another
flick in the opposite direction he gestures at Mendoza –
"Or is there some other game going on here we need to
discuss? Where did you get it? What's the money for?"

"It's my retirement fund," I gasp out from between my
bloody lips. "I'm moving to Amsterdam. Gonna buy a little
houseboat. Adopt a cat. Maybe grow a beard—"

This is more than he can take, apparently. He bursts
upright and hauls back with his foot and starts kicking me
as viciously as he can in my stomach and side. He's almost
apoplectic, with spittle flying from his lips as he screams at me.

"NO MORE fucking jokes! What the hell is wrong with
you? What kind of sick, messed-up shithead are you, you
dumb sumbitch?"

He tires of kicking me in the side and as I slowly slump
over sideways, coughing and choking on a mouthful of blood,
he delivers one more massive kick, this time to my temple,
and everything goes black once again.

*   *   *

I've never found before that waking up was a particularly
depressing experience, but as I regain consciousness I can't
help but feel pretty disappointed to once again be joining the

land of the living. My mouth tastes like a small animal has crawled inside and died in there, and my left hand throbs with a drumbeat of intense pain that's keeping time with my pulse. As much as I don't really want to open my eyes, I almost can't, anyways, as they are all but swollen shut. I think all my ribs are broken, and it's so painful to breathe I shudder in terror at how it would feel to cough. Need to avoid coughing at all costs, I remind myself. Need to avoid breathing, too, but I'm sure that won't be an issue for much longer.

Eventually, I venture to crack open my eyes as much as I can and scan the room. Tommy is sitting at the lunch counter, merrily humming away as he sorts the little stacks of bills, while Leon and Ice Pick are busy in the kitchen wrapping up Leon's shattered wrist in some dish towels. I can hear Leon yelping and cursing as Ice Pick tightly binds up the towels with a long strip of duct tape.

I swivel my head slightly to my right, wincing at the little shafts of pain that lance through my body from performing even just this little movement, and see that Mendoza has regained consciousness as well. He notices me looking at him, but doesn't say anything.

"For a moment I thought they'd killed you," I murmur quietly.

"For a moment, I thought they did, too," he whispers back. His voice sounds a lot weaker than the last time we spoke.

"What are you doing here?" I ask.

"I came for my money."

"You're early."

"I got impatient."

"And how did you even know I went and got it? I know I wasn't followed, unless you used a plane."

"No, nothing so elaborate," he says.

"Then how…."

He looks at me sideways and raises his eyebrows. Really? I thought you were a smart guy."

I close my eyes and try to concentrate. The answer is poking at the back of my brain. I just have to let it in.

"GPS," I say finally. "You put a tracker on my car. It's so obvious I missed it entirely."

He nods. "The simplest methods are usually the best. Did you really think I would let you drive around without following your every movement? I even know you stopped and got a coffee here before you headed off on your little field trip."

I say nothing in response. Hopefully, that's what everyone will keep thinking.

Tommy finally finishes counting the stacks of money and calls out, "Five hundred fifty thou. Exactly."

Ice Pick comes in and looks at the stacks skeptically.

"You sure? The guy said there should be almost one and a half mil."

"The rest must be somewhere else, then, boss. I counted it twice. Five hundred fifty. Not a penny more."

"Ah, *fangool,*" says Ice Pick quietly, then turns and looks at me.

"Where's the rest?" he says, walking up and standing over me. "You might as well give it up. You won't be needing money where you're going. Spill."

I cough out a pathetic imitation of a laugh (and immediately regret it) and say, "Look around you. You're standing in it. It's in the café. In the walls, in the benches, in the grill and the freezer. You think these things grow on trees?"

This revelation doesn't make him happy.

"I'm not buying it. My guy says this little shit stole a million euros from him. I don't know how much that is in real money, but I know it's a hell of a lot more than what's in that bag. And if that's all I take back to him, he'll have my head on a platter."

"Welcome to my world," I say.

"Maybe he's right, boss," says Leon quietly. "Could be this is all that's left."

"Don't be an idiot, Leon. Look around you – you think it cost almost a million bucks to fix up this dump? No friggin' way. A hundred thou, *tops*.

"I'll tell you what I think: I think this asshole was cleaning the money for the little French shithead, but he was getting it only a piece at a time. You wouldn't want to hand over your whole nut to one guy. You'd make multiple trips. This bag has just one part of the loot.

"And I'll tell you what else I think: I think the asshole's right. The money is all around us, but not the way he wants us to believe. How much you want to bet the cash really is in the walls and the benches and everywhere else he mentioned?"

He walks over to the far wall and rips down one of the framed paintings and flings it off to the side, then pounds his fist against the wall.

"It's in the walls, asshole. Those shitty paintings are just cover to hide patches in the plaster. We knock a few holes in the walls and we'll find some very expensive insulation inside them, you watch and see.'

He twists in a circle, looking for something to poke against the wall but there's nothing usable in sight.

"Tommy, go into the kitchen and get me something heavy. Look for one of those hammer things they use to pound meat."

"You mean a meat tenderizer."

"Yeah, whatever. Just go get something. And Leon, put that money back in the bag and stash it in the freezer in the kitchen. Hide it good."

When Tommy returns with a meat tenderizer Ice Pick starts hammering away at the wall, gradually punching a small hole into it, and then reaches into the hole and yanks back a large wedge of plaster. Peering inside, he grumbles something inaudibly, then straightens out and says, "Nothing here, but that just means we didn't get lucky the first time. There's a lot more wall in this place."

"There's no way we can tear this place apart with a meat tenderizer, boss," says Tommy, obviously worried that he will be the one tasked with demolishing the restaurant.

"Yeah, I agree. We'll have to go get a couple sledgehammers in the morning."

I glance over at Renault, who is showing more animation than I have seen in him since I arrived. The sight of his beloved café being demolished has obviously affected him greatly, and he's trembling and breathing heavily. His hands are scratching at the duct tape tying them to his belt, and little bubbles of blood are dripping from his mouth.

"Maybe it's not in the walls, boss," says Tommy, still holding out hope of escaping a day of exhausting manual labour. "Maybe it's in the benches, like the guy said."

And he disappears into the kitchen them immediately reappears holding a large butcher knife. Walking directly over to the nearest banquette, he plunges the knife directly down into the seat cushion and pulls it in a long line, opening up a huge gash in the vinyl. He drops the knife on the table and sticks his hands down into the gash and starts viciously ripping out stuffing, tossing it onto the floor behind him.

The sight is too much for Renault, who may have been able to endure being beaten and disfigured, but cannot tolerate the sight of the destruction being visited on his restaurant.

Exploding up from the floor like a duck bursting out of a pond, Renault launches himself in a fury at Tommy, who has his back to the room while he bends over and tears at the upholstery. I notice Renault has managed to tear his hands away from his belt but they're still bound tightly together. He lifts his arms up high and brings both fists down onto Tommy's back, who is taken completely by surprise by the sudden attack and falls face forward onto the banquette and is wedged between the seat and the table. Renault reaches his hands over to the butcher knife laying on the table and picks it up, gripping it tightly in both hands, and raises it up before bringing it down and skewering Tommy in the back.

His aim is off, though, and the blade barely penetrates, hitting Tommy in one of his shoulder blades. But before Renault can pull back and stab again, the top of his head shatters into a bloody explosion of blood and brain and skull, splattering against the newspapers taped over the window.

Ice Pick lowers his gun very slowly as Renault topples forward onto Tommy, who is still pinned down on the eviscerated banquette. A torrent of bodily fluids pulses out of what is left of Renault's head, gushing onto Tommy, who flails helplessly and wails, "Get him off! Get him off!"

Ice Pick walks up and grabs Renault's ankles, and pulls him backwards, dropping him face first onto the floor, where he lies motionless. Tommy scrambles backwards up off the banquette and tries to stand upright, but ends up stepping on Renault's corpse, which trips him up and sends him tumbling off to the side and onto the floor.

"Stop fooling around," says Ice Pick. "Look what you made me go and do. I didn't want to off him till he'd given up the rest of the loot. All that work for nothing. *Fanculo!* You better pray one of those other two shitheads can tell us what we need to know.

"I swear, you two guys are going to send me to an early grave. It's a mystery how you've managed to stay alive this long without my help."

Leon is still studiously stacking the bricks of cash in the duffel bag.

"Holy shit, Leon," says Ice Pick. "How friggin' long are you going take with that bag?"

"Sorry, boss, I was distracted by the floor show," he says, chuckling at the sight of a blood-soaked Tommy bending over trying to claw pieces of Renault's brain out of his hair.

Ice Pick grimaces in disgust, then leans down and grabs what's left of Renault's head by his hair, lifting his face up off the floor; he takes out his phone and snaps a picture of the dead man's mutilated face.

"I gotta send this to our guy. You two keep from dying for the next five minutes, OK? Think you can manage that?"

He walks into the kitchen and presses a button on his phone. Just before he steps outside the café I hear the long tones of a European phone ringing, then the door closes behind him.

The café has begun to resemble the set of a horror movie, with holes in the walls, torn-up furniture, blood and brains painted liberally across the scene, and a partially-decapitated corpse laying in the middle of it all.

"Wait a sec – what's this?" Leon says suddenly, looking closely at the duffel bag. "There's some kinda hidden pocket here, and look what's inside. It must be this asshole's wallet. No wonder we couldn't find one on him."

This comment puzzles me. If they couldn't find my wallet, then where in the world could it be? I clearly remember grabbing it and my phone and putting them both into the inside breast pocket of my suit jacket before I left my apartment.

With only one hand working, Leon can't look through the wallet, so Tommy takes it from him and starts pulling out the contents and spreading them on the counter. He grabs up one of the cards and walks over to me, holding up the card beside my face and looking back and forth comparing the two.

"It's hard to tell, after what you've done to this guy's kisser," he says, "But it looks like this is him, alright."

Leon is still sorting through the cards that Tommy has scattered on the counter and mumbles, "Hold on, what have we got here?" and picks up a small tan-coloured business card. He squints at it in the low light, holding it up to get a clearer look. As he reads it his expression gradually changes, taking on an air of alarm.

Leon walks over to Tommy, who is still perched over me, and wordlessly hands him the card. I can see it clearly as Tommy carefully examines it, holding it in front of his face and turning it over to read both sides.

On the front of the card it says merely, "Cammarata Social Club". On the back, handwritten in a careful, meticulous script, is the notation, "Please extend every courtesy to my nephew." It is signed, "Dominic Chiappetta".

"Mother of God," he says in a hushed voice. I can't tell from the tone whether he's praying or swearing.

"Do you know what we've done here?" says Leon. "This guy's a made man. And look who his uncle is."

"Son of a bitch," says Tommy quietly, holding the card reverently, the way you would handle a precious relic. "We've gotta tell Ice Pick about this."

"He's not gonna be happy."

"Yeah, well compare how unhappy he's going to be with how unhappy this guy's uncle will feel when he learns what we've done to his nephew. I don't think this is the kind of 'courtesy' he wants us to extend."

Mendoza is studying me carefully, obviously puzzled by this latest bit of news. He knows I'm not the beloved nephew of a major Mob boss and I can almost hear the wheels spinning in his head as he tries to figure out how I'm going to play this out.

Our thoughts are all interrupted by the explosive banging that thunders out again from the back door.

"For the last time, Leon, give Ice Pick the key you took off that asshole. I'm not some friggin' doorman," grumbles Tommy, as he hustles over to open the kitchen door.

When Ice Pick enters the room his mood looks even fouler than it was before. He strides directly over to Renault's body and delivers a tremendous kick that lifts it several inches up off the floor.

"You little shit!" he screams at the corpse. "If you were still alive I'd tear you apart piece by piece, you *fottuto stronzino!*"

He spins around and glares at Leon and Tommy. "The shit has really hit the fan now. If we don't find the rest of the money our guy is going to take it out of our hides. And you two idiots made me kill the one guy here who knows for sure where it is! Those other two are useless – I might as well off them both right this friggin' minute." Pulling out his gun, he strides purposely over to me and Mendoza.

"Ah, Ice Pick, before you do that, I think first you might wanna hear about something we found in the asshole's bag." Tommy's voice is filled with concern, and the big man turns around and glares at him.

"What?! What did you find? Is he a cop or something?"

"Um, no, we could deal with that. This is worse…" and he holds out to Ice Pick the little tan card from the social club. The big man stomps over to the counter and snatches the card from Tommy's hand and holds it up to the light to get a good look.

Even in the dim light it's easy to see the blood drain from Ice Pick's face as he carefully reads the card. His lips move silently as he reads the script again, then he looks over to me, then back to the card, then finally back over to me again.

Ice Pick steps over and leans forward, glaring at me.

"Do you have anything you'd like to say to me?"

"Yeah," I croak, pausing to let a large bubble of blood drip from my mouth, and doing my best to channel the spirit of the dead mobster in the motel. "You're a dead man."

I can't swear to it, but I think I hear Mendoza snort in amusement beside me. My material might be a little too hip for the room, but at least there's one person here who gets me.

"Why didn't you tell us you're a made guy?"

"It didn't come up."

"And now I suppose you think this makes a difference. That I'm suddenly just going to let you go and pat you on your back and send you on your merry way? You think this means anything to me? I'm just as Italian as you are, you got nothin' on me."

"You may be Italian, but you're not from Sicily," I say, trying to inject contempt into my voice. "If you were, you wouldn't be stuck sweating your ass off in Texas while the rest of us wops live the high life in places that actually matter. You're Italian alright, but you're garbage. You're the kind we use to run our errands and to pick up our dog shit. You're nothing but an errand boy right now, working for some frog in exchange for some shitty finder's fee. You wear expensive suits and brag about your nickname and you like to salt your speech with Italian words to remind the rest of us where you come from, but I'm a made man and you're just *cafone*. In case you don't know that one, I'll help you out – it means 'loser'."

Ice Pick's response is to haul off and backhand me viciously in the mouth with the barrel of his gun. My head whips to the side and I start to topple over but he reaches out and grabs me by my shoulder and pulls me back upright.

"Uh-uh," he says. "No more naptime for you, sweetheart.

I'm not done talking with you yet."

"*Vaffanculo*," I say through my bloody lips. "You may not be done with me, but I'm sure as fuck done with you. You have only one possible chance to escape this *disgrazia*. You had it right the first time: you let me and my partner stand up and walk right out of here, along with our money, of course, and if you're lucky, really, really fucking lucky like you've never been before, my uncle might just let you live. There'll be a price to pay, of course, but it doesn't have to be your life. But if you don't let us go, and I mean right this fucking second, you're crossing a line and there's no turning back."

I can tell he wants to hit me again. He's not used to being spoken to this way. But my words are sinking through. I can see in his eyes he's having second thoughts, and he's not happy about it.

Finally, though, some synapse in his brain snaps into place and you can see he's made a decision. His eyes get hard and he straightens up.

"Forget about it," he says. "Where I'm putting your body even the vultures won't find it. I got nothin' to worry about from you." And he turns around and rejoins his men at the counter.

I can hear Mendoza quietly chuckling beside me.

"Well, it was worth a try," I grumble. "I'm glad to see you find it so funny."

"I just like how you've been screwing with the big loudmouth," he says quietly. "That takes real *cojones*. It's fair to say my estimation of you has greatly increased."

"Thanks for the compliment, but I still don't like you."

"I'm used to it," he answers. "Where did you learn all that Italian stuff?"

"I spent two years hanging out on the docks in Brindisi. My Italian's probably better than that goombah's. Plus, I saw *Goodfellas*. Didn't work, though."

"I see I made a mistake earlier – those boys in the motel, you didn't know them at all, did you? But then why were they here to begin with?"

"Your people probably aren't the only ones Willie had a conversation with. I'm betting they came down to straighten out whoever's been besmirching their good name."

"So then it's your fault I'm in this mess."

"I don't think so. You wouldn't be in this position if your pigheaded pride hadn't forced you to squeeze me for money. You even said yourself that it was a trivial sum. You should have gone through the regular channels and sorted things out like a civilised man. You don't poke the bear."

"That's not how we do things where I grew up," he says, then sighs heavily. "You may be right, though. I can tend to be a little, ah, overzealous."

"Is that what you call executing two Mob hitmen in a motel room? 'Overzealous'?"

"I don't think you fully appreciate my position. I have people above me. I have even more people below me. I have to keep the upper levels satisfied while sufficiently intimidating the lower ones. It can get overwhelming at times."

"That job would never work for me. I've never been a team player."

He sighs heavily again, then says, "Apparently I'm not much of one, either."

My little speech must have gotten to Ice Pick, because he's starting to look worried. I'm still holding out hope he'll crack

under the strain and actually set us loose, but that hope gets
a little fainter once he starts grilling Tommy about where
to dump our bodies.

"So you're sure this is good information?"

"Yeah, yeah, it's solid," says Tommy enthusiastically.
"The guy I know says it's perfect – right off a good road
but out of sight, and totally deserted. And about forty feet
straight down."

"I dunno, Tommy, I never used an abandoned well before.
What if a hurricane comes through and they float to the
surface?"

"Forty feet, Ice Pick! The freakin' Gulf of Mexico could
flood this place and it still might not be enough to fill a
forty foot well. I'm telling you, once they go down that hole
they're *never* coming back up."

"OK, I'm sold. We'll use the asshole's car. We can stuff
their bodies in the trunk. It's big enough. No way I want their
blood and guts all over my upholstery – I just had that thing
detailed."

Ice Pick turns his head to look over at Mendoza and me
and I don't like the look I see in his eyes. It's cold and hard,
and speaks of imminent violence.

Walking over to us, he stands looking down, a towering,
menacing shape. I focus my eyes on his shoes, and note with
satisfaction that their perfect polish is marred with little
spatters of blood. It somehow diminishes him, reducing him
to a mere thug in a nice suit.

He squats down on his haunches in front of the little
Mexican, and says, "Now. What about you? What have you
got for me that might convince me you're worth keeping
alive?"

I don't think he cares for the response, as Mendoza's reply is succinct, and consists of a fat glob of spittle and blood, which he spits with perfect accuracy directly into the big man's face.

"*Pendejo.*" Mendoza says the word with a tone of finality. I have to admire his spirit.

The big man straightens up then slowly reaches into his jacket breast pocket and pulls out a white handkerchief, which he then presses very carefully against his mouth and chin and wipes them clean.

"Now I have something for you," he says quietly. "You dirty, greasy, nasty little wetback scum." And raising his gun, he calmly pulls the trigger and puts two little holes in the Mexican's forehead. A fat splatter of blood and brains appears immediately behind the little man, splashing against the wall and slowly dripping down out of sight behind his shoulders.

I'm ready for it, and determined not to give him the satisfaction of even so much as blinking in his direction, but to my surprise he pockets his gun and says, "You don't get off so easy, asshole. I got something *special* in mind for you.

"Ever been dropped down a forty-foot well? I'm hoping the fall don't kill you, because I want to think about you tonight laying in a heap with two corpses, while the rats and scorpions feast on you. With any luck, it might be days before you finally die, screaming in agony."

And he straightens back up, smooths out his trousers, and gives a little laugh before turning around and walking away.

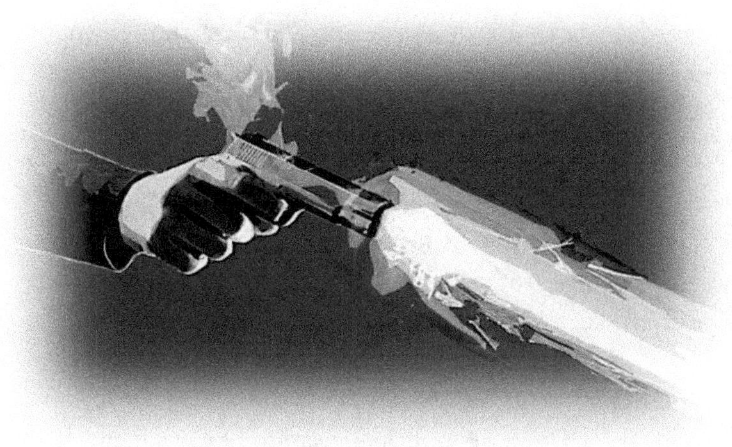

THE ICEMAN COMETH

TOMMY STUFFS ME into the trunk of my car while Leon cradles his broken wrist and offers helpful suggestions. He wedges me deep in the space then disappears back into the café leaving Leon to stand watch, making sure that somehow I don't regain control of my body and scramble out and run away. It's a nice thought, but right now all my strength is being used up just trying to keep breathing. Which gets even harder once Tommy returns and dumps Renault's dripping corpse onto me, and then follows it up a minute later with Mendoza's.

I'm crammed into a little pocket far forward in the trunk, choking on the stench of dead body and fresh blood, when

Tommy slams it shut to leave me crushed beneath the two corpses in total darkness. Little pit-pats tapping away on the trunk lid tell me the rain has picked up a bit in strength, but it still sounds pretty weak. I hope these guys didn't leave my car windows open. The leather seats don't like to get wet.

Nothing more happens for what seems like an eternity and I lay there gasping for every breath and wondering how much longer I can keep it up, then suddenly I hear the sound of footsteps on the gravel outside, and the car bouncing as two heavy bodies settle into the front seats, and finally the sound of the engine starting up and the sensation of movement.

I'm already wondering if I'll suffocate before we get to our destination when a particularly bad jolt from hitting a bump in the road lifts the two bodies off me and moves them closer to the back bumper, giving me a bit of breathing room and a chance to actually move my arms around.

There's nothing in the trunk that I could use to defend myself, but even if there were a machine gun here I doubt I'd have the strength to use it. It does occur to me that there is a thick wad of cash tucked away just beside my head, and for no good reason, I manage to reach up and pull it out from underneath the felt covering and stuff it down into my pants pocket. I reflect that it's a wasted effort because, as Ice Pick so kindly pointed out, I won't be needing any money where I'm going. I'd still rather have it with me than leave it for these guys, though. Maybe I can use it to pay the ferryman.

But that small burst of exertion drains out of me what little strength I had remaining, and I decide it's easier to just lay back and await the inevitable conclusion of this one-way trip.

I suppose I passed out at some point in the journey, because suddenly I'm staring into the nuclear blaze of a flashlight beam shining into the trunk. We must have reached our destination, and Tommy is grunting with effort as he tugs on Mendoza's limp form, eventually managing to free it from the trunk and letting it drop down onto the dirt.

"I don't suppose I'm going to get any help from you at all," he grumbles to Leon, who is standing back holding the flashlight. "You would have to go and screw up your arm just before the hard work begins."

"You think I like this?" Leon hollers. "I wish Ice Pick hadn't gone and offed this little shithead before I had a chance to teach him a good fucking lesson!" And he walks over to the corpse and starts viciously kicking it in the side.

"Shit, Leon, calm down. He's not feelin' it, man. You're just wearing yourself out."

"Yeah? Well it feels good, all the same."

From where I lay in the trunk I can see the rain coming down pretty hard now, as a glistening shaft of raindrops twinkles in the beam from Leon's flashlight.

Tommy bends down then disappears from sight and I can hear him grunting with effort as he drags the body away into the night.

Leon comes up to the trunk and shines the flashlight beam directly into my eyes, chuckling as I wince and turn my head to the side.

"Wassamatta, dickhead? What happened to the smart mouth? Not feelin' so clever now, are you?"

"Shouldn't you go help your girlfriend?" I croak back at him. "He's probably already pissed that you're going to have to learn to jerk him off with your left hand now."

I have to chuckle, as he is helpless to respond effectively, since he'd have trouble reaching me where I'm tucked away deep in the trunk sheltered by another body. He just gurgles incoherently and then says, "You think about that while you're laying at the bottom of that well," and he turns away and disappears into the blackness of the night.

I'm wondering if there's any possibility of me crawling free and stumbling away when Tommy finally comes back and starts tugging on Renault's corpse. Tommy is soaked pretty good, and his hair is matted down in a wet mass and dripping onto his suit, which looks soaked through.

"Friggin' rain," complains Leon behind him. "364 days a year it's bone dry out here but when we show up suddenly it's monsoon season."

"Why don't you just go sit in the car then, you pussy," grunts Tommy, hefting Renault out of the trunk and letting him fall onto the ground like a sack of potatoes. "You're no friggin' help anyways."

"And who'd make sure the asshole don't run away while you're dropping bodies into wells?"

"Hell, Leon, look at the guy. I'm surprised he's still breathing, let alone capable of any kind of movement. Ice Pick kicked him so long I thought he was going to wear out his shoe."

"Yeah, well I'm not taking any chances. Hurry up and dump that guy so the real fun can begin."

Without Renault's body in the way I see if maybe I can drag myself into a better position in the trunk, but Tommy was right; my whole chest shrieks in pain if I budge even an inch and I suspect that several of my broken ribs are stabbing into my lungs; the pain coming from where I think my kidneys are lances through me like jabs from a red-hot poker and my head throbs so bad I'm almost blind from the headache. I'm exhausted and in agony, and to tell the truth, ready to give up. I hope the fall into the well kills me immediately.

I'm laying there, staring up into the night, when an assassin bug lands with a silent flutter on the lip of the trunk, and sits there looking directly at me. His little antennae twitch soundlessly as he tastes the night air and assesses the panoply of smells emanating from the various spilled fluids and body parts that drench the trunk. He raises his wings slightly away from his body and then lowers them again, as though he was going to fly away and then changed his mind. Or maybe he's just showing off, teasing me by demonstrating that he can leave this place whenever he wants, unlike the big dumb earthbound humans.

"Alright for you, buddy," I mumble. "You can have your little laugh. Bet your girlfriend's not as cute as mine, though." And I cough out a pathetic chuckle at my own joke.

The bug doesn't think my joke is very funny, and in response he chooses to fly away, and I can hear the buzz of his departure as he zings off into the rain.

It seems to take even longer for Tommy to return this time, and when he gets back he's a complete mess. He's added a generous helping of blood to the rainwater that's drenched his suit, and he's walking funny.

"What the hell happened to you?" says Leon, gaping wide-eyed at Tommy.

"I almost fell down the fucking well, is what happened to me, you useless tit! That little shithead's belt got caught on my watchband and almost pulled me in after him! If the band hadn't broken I'd probably be down there right now, no thanks to you!

"And on the way back I stepped into some kind of gopher hole or snake hole and it sucked the shoe right off my freakin' foot! And then in the rain and the dark I couldn't find the hole to get my shoe back – it's like the earth closed up again and swallowed it.

"Plus I lost my goddamned watch."

Leon can't contain his laughter, and this enrages Tommy even more.

"And I'll tell you one other thing: there is no way in Hell I'm dragging that asshole over there by myself. It wouldn't surprise me at all if I ended up at the bottom and he was left to piss down all over me."

"What're we gonna do then? We can't take him back with us."

"I'll tell you what we're doing. We drag his sorry ass out of there and dump him into the ditch then put a round into the back of his skull. The vultures will pick him clean before anyone finds him, and he'll end up just another nameless dead guy sitting in the county morgue. Probably the tenth one this week."

"I dunno, Tommy. Ice Pick was pretty clear…."

"Then let Ice Pick come drag the asshole across this mudfield. I didn't sign up for this. Either you drag him to that well yourself or we off him here. It's your choice."

"Fine. We do him here. Can you at least pull him out of there?"

Tommy leans into the trunk to grab hold of me and I decide the time has come to punch him forcefully in the face, maybe knock a few of his own teeth down his throat, and I launch my fist out in an explosive burst.

"Haw haw, look, Leon! He's fighting back!"

And I realise the explosive burst of my fist is actually merely a pathetic little twitching that barely waggles my hand out in Tommy's general direction, and I bow to the inescapable truth that my best fighting days are behind me.

"C'mon, dickhead, stop embarrassing yourself. Take it like a man." And pulling my sleeve, he tugs me toward him and rolls me over the lip of the trunk and lets me fall onto the ground.

If I thought I was in pain before, this latest move really puts the lie to that. I can't even bring myself to groan, it hurts so bad. I feel myself being dragged across the pavement, then over gravel, and then finally rolled into some kind of ditch off to the side of the road. I come to a stop laying face down in the mud and weeds, sucking up air through a little raised patch of soil.

"I suppose I have to do this too—" I hear Tommy say, and then Leon interrupts him.

"Oh no you don't. This one's mine. I been waiting for this all night. Don't think I can't fire this thing with my left."

If these two guys had spent more than a few hours in this county they'd recognise the sound that even I can hear from my position on the ground. It starts quietly, almost like a whisper, and then gradually sharpens and builds in volume, until it becomes a droning, rasping buzz like a model airplane on steroids that's heading right for us.

"Bye bye, sweetheart," I hear Leon say, but then instead of a loud bang I hear in rapid progression the sickening smack of a spiky proboscis impacting with the back of someone's neck, a sharp, sudden exclamation of pain and anger, and lastly that bang I had been expecting. Pain lances through the top of my skull as I feel something burning a line through my hair.

"Oh my holy FUCK!" shrieks Leon, and I can hear him falling back into the muck as his foot slips out from under him.

"What the hell just hit my neck?" he hollers. I can hear the sickening crunch of the assassin bug's body as he reaches up behind himself and yanks the bug off his neck and crushes it into paste in his fist.

It's Tommy's turn to laugh now, and I can hear him howling convulsively at his partner's distress. Leon is yelping in pain as the full effect of the bug's toxins seep into his flesh and enter his system.

"Help me up, asshole, and stop laughing! I think I need to go to the hospital – what the hell just attacked me?"

"We'll never know now," says Tommy. "Whatever it was once, it's just mush now. Don't be such a baby. Let's get the fuck out of here. I've had enough of this place to last me for the rest of my life."

"You got nothin' on me, Tommy. I been sick of this shithole since we got here."

I can hear them stumbling away in the night, one of them obviously limping and the other dragging his feet as though he's drugged, and then the sound of two car doors slamming, and they drive away.

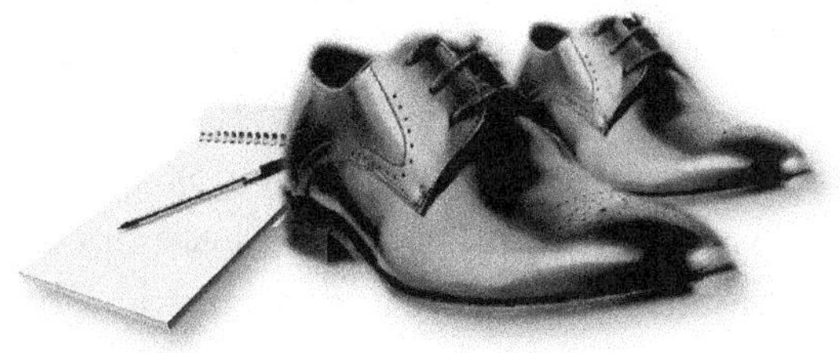

MR. District ATTORNEY

 **Y MIND** wakes up before my eyes do. I am in no hurry to lift my eyelids and instead lie there motionless, letting my ears take in all the information I need to know.

The rhythmic quiet beeping coming from somewhere off to my side comforts me with its metronomic reassurance that my heart and lungs are still working as they should, and the throbbing in my legs and sides tells me that I'm not paralysed.

Some unpleasant busybody synapse in my consciousness nags at me that I might well be paralysed after all and just experiencing phantom pain, so with superhuman effort I force myself to bend my leg and to lift my knee high enough to disturb the covers over my chest. I feel the sheet slipping down from my chin and I let my leg collapse back onto the bed. Mission Accomplished.

I don't know how I got here, and I don't remember much of what happened once I arrived, except for isolated snippets – brief flashes of random images that appear sporadically and disappear just as quickly. The doctors bending over me, their concerned, quietly competent faces focusing downwards in my direction; the pretty, blonde candy-striper dabbing a wet cloth to my parched lips; the efficient nurses who sweep in and out of my room, checking the machines and adjusting the various tubes emerging from various places on my body.

I'm in no hurry to make sense of it all. Whenever I slip back into consciousness my brain decides the time isn't right just yet, and the lights go out again. And all I know is the bed is comfortable, and I'm feeling no pain.

*   *   *

It's during one such brief episode of consciousness when I hear the approach of quiet footsteps in the corridor outside my room. With a prescient sixth-sense premonition I know those footsteps are headed for me, and I hope against hope that they belong to that pretty little candy-striper coming to give me a sponge bath. It's such moments that get us through the day.

I hear the footsteps enter my room and stop at the side of my bed. I venture to crack open one of my eyes, looking for a spray of blonde hair framing bubblegum-pink lipstick, but am greeted instead by the sight of a dark suit, dark eyes, dark hair, and no lipstick at all.

The man who stands hovering beside my bed is in his early 40's, wearing a sensible charcoal-grey suit, nice but not showy, a white shirt with a tightly-knotted blue tie, and from what I'd heard earlier, sensible shoes. Nature has blessed him with what some might call a chiseled jawline. He is clean-shaven and looks serious. A police detective if I ever saw one.

I am wrong though. Same job, but different department. When he sees I am awake and looking at him he introduces himself: Carl Crawford, Ector County District Attorney.

"District Attorney," I rasp. "I'm flattered. Or is it just a slow news day?"

He chuckles good-naturedly. "Bit of both, actually.

"It *has* been a little quiet around these parts, lately, but you're a curious case, and I wanted to meet for myself the man who gets beaten within an inch of his life but still has four thousand dollars in his pocket when we find him."

I smile slightly when I hear this.

"Well, I guess every cloud does have its silver lining, after all," I croak. "Doesn't really make everything all better, but I'll take what I can get."

"Mm-hm," he replies, watching me closely as if he were trying to figure out a puzzle. "But it makes a person wonder, don't you know, why someone did what they did to you – and I've got to assume it took more than one guy – why they did that and left you with a wad of centuries that could choke a horse. They must have had a reason that had nothing to do with money."

"You're overlooking the obvious," I say, all but whispering so that he has to incline his head slightly to catch all my words. "My car. They wanted my car. I was carjacked."

"Your car. Someone beat you all the way to Hell and back and all they wanted was your car? Was it made of solid gold?"

"No. But it was a classic. Obviously, they're collectors."

"And what kind of car was this?" he asks, pulling a little pen and notebook out of his jacket's inside breast pocket.

"Um, it was a 2002 Buick LeSabre. Four-door. Brown. Bit of rust."

"A LeSabre," he repeats after me, flatly.

"Yeah."

"And what can you tell me about this LeSabre?"

"Um, let's see. I can describe it. Hold on…. Brown interior, leather seats. Burns oil a bit. Right passenger window won't go down and there's a big hole in the dash above the glove compartment from where the air bags deployed once. Um, gas gauge doesn't work… now that I think about it, none of the other instruments in the dash work, either. The speedometer's still OK, though. Oh – and the rear springs are shot. Back end bounces like crazy when you hit a bump.

"Other than that, she's mint."

He's not smiling anymore. He lets loose a long heavy sigh and lowers the pen and notebook.

"You know, if you didn't want to tell me what really happened, you could have just told me so right out. Saved us both a bit of time."

"You've got me all wrong, Counselor. There's nothing I like better than to be a helpful citizen. Everything's still all hazy in my mind, though. All I remember is a bunch of guys and about a hundred fists. Everything else is just a blur."

"Well then, why don't you fill me in on the parts that aren't a blur, like your name and birth date and where you live and how you make a living?"

I bring him up to speed on my vital statistics, but when it comes to describing my current form of income his attention perks up.

"'Master Tradesman'," he says. "Which means what, exactly?"

"Well, right now it means I'm between engagements, actually. But in the meantime I can probably help you fix whatever little problems are giving you grief. You know the routine: plumbing repairs, computer tune-up, pour a new concrete patio, pest removal. That sort of thing."

"Do you think maybe this little altercation you had might have been the result of some recent work you were doing? Maybe some 'pest removal', perhaps?"

"It would take a hell of a lot of cockroaches to kick my ass this badly, I'm pretty sure."

"I was thinking more of the two-legged variety of pest."

"That's out of my league, Mr. District Attorney. That sort of stuff I leave to you and your boys."

"Mm-hm," he replies skeptically.

"Say, Counselor, I was wondering if you might do me a little favour. Might even turn out to be a reciprocal agreement – I think I may have some information for you that you'd really enjoy hearing."

"And what would you be needing from me in the meantime?"

"Nothing particularly valuable. I was just hoping you could keep from running my name through your computer right away. I kinda suspect it might benefit me if certain parties were to think I'm dead."

"And exactly who might these 'certain parties' be?"

"Uh-uh. That's part of the information I'm offering."

"Precisely. Or maybe you're unclear about the definition of 'reciprocal'."

"Not at all, but my information isn't ready for sharing, yet. It's more of a work in progress, but I can promise you'll like the final product."

"I don't know. You're asking a lot without giving me much in return. If you check out of here before I can run your particulars, and it turns out you've fed me a line of bullshit, I'll look like an idiot."

"Well, if you promise to keep it on the QT, I can give you a couple of character references that should calm your fears somewhat."

"You think I would be satisfied because you've got a couple of buddies who are willing to lie for you?"

"If one of them is the American Ambassador to Denmark, and the other is the Senior Vice President and General Counsel to the World Bank, then yeah, maybe."

"And how would an unemployed handyman living in a Texas dusthole know these people?"

"We used to be roommates at boarding school in Gstaad, in Switzerland. We're still pretty close. I haven't actually had them over for dinner recently, but they'll vouch for me, all the same."

"Just *who* are you, anyways?" he says, scratching his head and looking at me intently, as though he's hoping to spot a zipper that he can pull to reveal another identity hiding beneath my outer shell.

"You said it yourself Counselor – just an unemployed handyman living in a Texas dusthole."

"Mm-hm." That skeptical tone is in his voice again. "Well, you haven't committed any crimes that I know of, so I suppose I can extend you this little courtesy," he says, and I wince internally at the turn of phrase; it brings back some nasty memories.

A stern-looking nurse in a crisply-pressed uniform appears in the doorway behind his shoulder and clears her throat meaningfully. He looks over at her and grimaces, then says, "Judging by the arrival of Nurse Ratched, looks like it's naptime for you again, my friend. Give me those names and I'll make some quiet phone calls. I'll look in on you again later. Maybe when your memory improves. If it improves."

"Anything's possible," I croak, grinning. "Take care now, Mr. District Attorney."

"It's Carl."

"Hmm?" I grunt, looking up at him.

"Call me 'Carl'. The only people who call me 'Mr. District Attorney' are the ones I'm prosecuting for committing crimes."

"Then it'll be 'Carl' from now on, as far as I'm concerned."

"Let's both of us hope so. See you again soon."

As he passes the nurse on his way out of my room I hear her say, "You know, I don't appreciate that 'Nurse Ratched' comment."

I can hear his laugh echoing as he walks away down the hallway on those sensible shoes of his.

*   *   *

When you're lying in a hospital bed, drugged to the rafters, and your only entertainment is following with your eyes the dust motes floating through a sunbeam that slowly traverses the room like a slow-motion spotlight sweeping the grounds of a secure compound, you can lose track of time.

At some point, a person wearing a long white coat over green scrubs comes up to my bed and smiles down at me and asks the stupidest question I've heard in quite a while.

"How are we doing today?" he says cheerfully, as though he's somehow managed to overlook the multitude of tubes and wires emerging from a dozen different parts of my body.

He might be older than 12 years old, but I can't tell for sure. He has thick, wavy, reddish-blond hair, a smattering of freckles tastefully scattered across his cheeks, and two large ears that stick out from either side of his head like miniature satellite dishes ready to scan the cosmos for signs of intelligent life.

My eyes won't focus so I can't read the badge on his coat to learn if he's a doctor, an intern, a nurse, or just the guy who mops the floor. He's got the eager, optimistic eyes of youth: bright eyes that haven't yet been dulled by an unending stream of images revealing the vast scale of human misery; idealistic eyes that suggest that hope still lives within his breast, not yet crushed beneath the weight of a cynical world. He smiles at me as though we've both just completed a particularly exhilarating roller coaster ride and he can't wait to get to the next one.

"I'm feeling OK," I say, in a voice that crawls out of my throat like a scarab beetle scratching its way out of a dusty tomb.

"It's the drugs," he says, and chuckles heartily. If he gets any happier he'll probably have to break into song.

"That will be ending soon, though," and for the first time he doesn't look like he's offering me an all-expense-paid trip for two to Maui. "We can't have you getting addicted.

"But that's good news," he says, brightening up again and resuming his Pollyanna impression, "You don't need them. There's not really anything wrong with you. We're sending you home."

"Are you sure you're in the right room?"

Again the hearty chuckle. "Sure am! Now, you probably feel like warmed-over poop, and there's no denying you had a pretty-good working over, including dislocating your shoulder and – judging by the swelling and redness – possibly fracturing your left ankle. But aside from two broken fingers on your left hand, several cracked ribs, contusions on both your eyes and a broken nose, you have no major broken bones, no damaged organs, no puncture wounds, and all your internal bleeding has stopped.

"Oh – you do have a pretty good gash on the top of your head. Best guess is something scraped you pretty bad. Maybe a bullet," he adds, in a slightly reproachful tone. "But none of that requires you to stay here in our lovely facility. All you need are a few days rest in your own bed, maybe some chicken soup and dry toast, and you'll be as good as new."

"'As good as new'."

"—Oh, I forgot to mention," he adds, glancing down at the iPad he's holding, "You probably have a concussion, as well. So try to avoid sports and video games for the next few days."

"Darn. You mean I'll have to drop out of the racquetball and Call of Duty tournaments this weekend?"

He looks momentarily alarmed, then gets the joke and bursts into hearty laughter. I'm sure he'll be repeating it later to his co-workers before his mommy comes to pick him up.

"Well," I croak, blinking my eyes hard, trying to focus, "Guess I'll be moving along then. Can I have a few minutes to gather my strength before I get up?"

"Oh, no, I think I misled you – we're sending you home alright, but not today. I just wanted to bring you the good news tonight. You don't have to leave until 8am tomorrow morning. But no more drugs for you!" And he reaches up and twists a little dial on a thin tube feeding into one of my IVs.

"Have a nice night," he chirps, then turns and bounces out of my room, on his way to brighten the next patient's day, maybe by telling them he's naming a new disease after them.

*　　　　*　　　　*

Displaying remarkably bad timing, Carl returns about two hours later, just when the painkillers have all but completely worn off and the full effect of my injuries is announcing itself to my brain in no uncertain terms.

"You don't look so good," he says, frowning down at me.

"They turned off the drugs," I moan. "Carl, do me a favour – you see that little dial on that tube there, can you give it a really big twist for me, do you think?"

He chuckles and says, "Now, now, you know better than that. You don't want to become a junkie like your friend Willie, now, do you?"

I'm not so out of it that I can't see him watching me intently, looking for my reaction to his comment. But if he thinks I'm going to jump up and tear my hair and shout "Oh no! How did you figure it out?", he's got a big disappointment coming.

"Willie?" I croak quietly. "Who? You have me at a disadvantage, Counselor."

He sighs quietly, then says, "So that's how we're playing this one, is it? Of course, I expected as much, but hope springs eternal, right? Had to ask.

"It's not even my case. But I did read Willie's statement and he tells a riveting story about being set up by a mysterious stranger from the St. Louis Mafia, and his description of the fellow sounds like this guy is your twin."

"Then I feel sorry for him, based on what I saw in the mirror this afternoon."

Carl chuckles, and says, "I think he might resemble the pre-Apocalypse version of you, more than today's sad edition."

"Thanks for the compliment. Does that mean you want me in a lineup now?"

"Oh heavens, no! No one's taking Willie's mysterious 'tall dark stranger' fantasy seriously. Especially since we searched his place and found plenty more incriminating evidence. Far as the Justice Department is concerned, the safety of our community can only benefit from the lack of guys like Willie on the streets. If someone really did set him up, they did us a favour."

"Plus, don't forget," I add, "There's an election coming up. Big drug busts are always a nice addition to any law-and-order candidate's campaign literature."

"I don't remember mentioning anything about a big drug bust," he says, smiling.

"No, but you said this fellow is a junkie, and he was set up to take him off the streets. I have to assume that doesn't mean he was caught shoplifting a candy bar at the Piggly Wiggly."

He chuckles good-naturedly, then snaps back into his serious mode. "So I was wondering if you're ready to share some of that information with me that you mentioned in our last conversation."

"You still need to wait until I can get my facts nailed down, Carl. I really haven't had much chance to do a lot of research while lying in this hospital bed. But this might cheer you up: they're cutting me loose. Tomorrow at 8am."

He raises an eyebrow in surprise, then takes a step back to assess me a bit more fully.

"They're discharging you? How? In a hearse?"

That makes me laugh so hard I wince. My sides don't like the exercise.

"They say there's nothing wrong with me. Just want me to ease up a bit on the sports for now."

"Wow. Well, I suppose we can attribute it to either the miracle of modern medical science, or the sorry state of our health insurance system – hospital beds don't grow on trees, you know. How are you getting home? Do you need a ride?"

"Nah, it's OK. I know a guy."

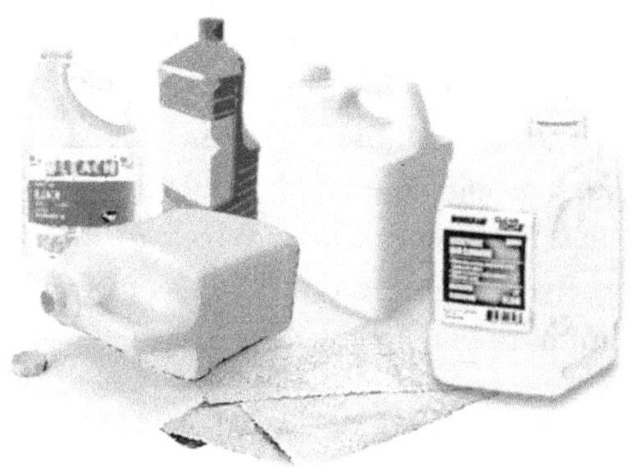

fun with science

JORGE SHOWS UP early, appearing in my hospital room at 7am, looking beside himself with worry and concern.

"*Hijo de la bruja!* What happened to you?" he exclaims, his eyes like saucers.

"I wouldn't pay for my Girl Scout cookies. The troop got angry."

"Well, it can't be too bad. You still have your sense of humour."

"It looks worse than it is, at least that's what they tell me."

This morning some kind old lady from the local chapter of the Salvation Army brought a set of clothes for me since the ones I'd arrived wearing were fit only for the incinerator, and argued with me for ten minutes before she finally broke down and agreed to accept a $100 donation in exchange. Then she made me wait for ten minutes while she painstakingly wrote out a receipt so I could deduct it from my taxes. Of course, that would mean I'd also have to add an entry for $4,000 received "from dead mobster's pocket", so I dropped the receipt in the wastebasket after she left.

*   *   *

Jorge helps me into the wheelchair that a nurse has brought, and he wheels me through the hospital and out the front doors and into the parking lot, where he proceeds to head directly for a big black SUV with tinted windows. He has to hold the chair tightly to keep it from tipping over as I surge up and try to leap out when I see the SUV.

"What's that doing here?" I scream, and yank ferociously on the wheels of my chair to twist it away.

"Hey, hey, calm down, amigo – that's our ride. I drove it out here for you. You said you need new wheels."

When we get closer I can see that the vehicle has Texas plates, which helps my heart rate to slow down to below 200. He stops at the passenger door and helps me up into the seat and I exhale deeply again as I note that there are no little decals on the windshield from any Houston parking garages.

I'm almost back to normal when my eyes catch sight of the key fob dangling from the ignition. Hanging alongside the fob, glinting unmistakably in the sunlight, is a little metal tag embossed with the Italian flag.

"Jorge!" I holler. "WHERE did you get this vehicle?"

"Well, that's actually a pretty funny story," he says, chuckling quietly. "You ever meet the guy who runs the motel on the road out of town? Name is Tex, or Rex, or Max… I dunno, I can never remember… It's something short like that, maybe—"

"Forget about his name!" I howl. "Why do you have this car?"

"Oh, well, as I was saying, this guy—" and he's about to start up the name game again until he catches sight of me and quickly switches back to the story. "Anyways, this guy from the motel shows up at my place the other afternoon with this car and asks me how much I'll give him for it.

"Well, of course I need to see the registration, but he doesn't have it. Says he 'lost' it. Right.

"So obviously I can't take it, but just as I'm opening my mouth to tell him to shove off, what do I see but a flatbed truck pulling up to my yard carrying a crumpled lump of steel that used to be a car.

"You know Red's boy? The oldest one who's at A&M? It was his birthday last week."

"Jorge! The car! Focus!"

"Hey, relax, good buddy – I'm getting to it. Just listen to this: this kid, he's so spoiled. His daddy got him a brand-new SUV for his birthday, and what does the little shit do? Drives it straight into an oil derrick at 80 miles an hour two days ago. Probably the first time the kid has ever driven in the rain. Doesn't have a clue. Doesn't understand how slippery the roads get when the rain starts falling and draws the oil up out of the pavement. Loses control on a corner and wham!

"Now, Red doesn't want anyone to know what the kid did – I think alcohol was involved, if you get me – so he wants me to just dispose of the wreck as quietly as possible without telling the cops or the insurance company, and writes me up a bill of sale. All perfectly legal, right?

"And the best part is, I got a receipt to show the IRS for the car—"

"Jorge, none of this explains—"

"Hey, I'm coming to it. You're gonna love this part, now. This SUV the kid was driving – it's the same make, model and year as the SUV the guy from the motel was trying to sell me. The two cars probably came off the same line within a couple months of each other.

"So what do I do? I gave the motel guy five hundred for it – told him I knew what was up and he's lucky I don't call the cops on him, and he grabs the money and he's gone before my office door has finished swinging shut.

"I swapped this car's VIN tag with the one I pulled off the kid's dash and switched license plates and *¡he ahí!* You got yourself a brand-new SUV for five hundred smackers, my friend!

"There's still a tag on the engine block," I say.

"When was the last time you got stopped for speeding and the cop pulled out your engine block?"

I look at the little Italian flag hanging on the key ring and I shudder, but I have to admit, it sounds like a pretty sweet deal.

"Crazy coincidence having both of these vehicles show up at the same time, though," he says. "Life sure is strange sometimes, isn't it?"

You have no idea, mi amigo. You have absolutely no idea.

*   *   *

Jorge drives us to his salvage yard and I force him to take two thousand dollars from me for the car. I almost have to hold him down to do it, but finally he relents and lets me give him the money.

Somehow, he's figured out this may be the last time we ever see each other, and there are tears in his eyes as he hugs me and says goodbye. There are tears in my eyes, too, but mostly because Jorge is hugging me so hard.

I've got no time for long weepy farewells, though, and after promising he'll be the first one I call the next time I need help, I slip into the driver's seat and head out of town.

On the way to my little hut I decide to take a little detour and I drive down the road that runs past Jenny's farm. Her place looks peaceful and undisturbed, sleeping peacefully in the sun like a little oasis in the desert. I continue on the road all the way until it meets the main highway, then turn south again and proceed to the shed. When I turn off the highway and onto the dirt track I notice with pleased satisfaction how smooth the formerly bumpy ride now seems.

When I get there I walk around the shed and up to the oil drum behind it, approaching with caution and hesitantly peering down into it. It appears devoid of any animate residents, but I'm not about to be fooled again. I very carefully tilt it over onto its side and lift the base up just enough to allow the contents to slide gently out onto the dirt.

I pick up the jugs of chemicals and load them into the back of the SUV, then return and set the drum back upright. I am about to turn away when I notice a flash of light in the

weeds. I walk over for a closer look and grunt in surprise.
My wallet and my phone are laying on the ground beside
a small wild juniper bush. Just where they would be if they
fell out of the breast pocket of someone standing near the
oil drum who tumbled face first into the dirt.

This is turning into a good day. I tuck them into my
pants pocket and head back to my vehicle.

I'm already feeling pretty exhausted and I want to grab
some rest before tonight's festivities, so I drive down to
Pecos and check into a small motel on the outskirts of town.
The lady at the desk doesn't mind taking cash from me at all,
especially when I decline a receipt.

There's a Walmart in this town and before settling in I
drive over there and buy a phone charger, a cordless electric
drill, a small bottle of isopropyl alcohol, a big fat potato and
a cheap towel, then head to my room. Once my phone comes
back to life I see that I have seventeen missed calls.
All from Jenny. I need to call her, but not until later tonight.
I just don't have the strength to deal with it right now.

*   *   *

When you try to kill someone, you cross a line.
And the rules are different on the other side of that line.
Actions I would never before have contemplated all seem
quite reasonable to me now.

As I lay back on the motel room bed, letting my eyes settle
on the mottled age stains on the ceiling above me, my mind
wanders. I run through the basics of the plan that I've worked
out, cross-checking for mistakes or miscalculations, but never
questioning the morality of any of it. Ice Pick and Leon and
Tommy didn't merely cross a line, they dragged me over it

along with them. In one sense they really did kill me
when they left me lying in that ditch. And they replaced me
with someone else.

I sit up on the bed and gobble a handful of the pills
the hospital gave me before they gave me the boot.
The pills don't really take away much of the pain, but
I don't want them to, really. The pain is keeping me going.
Without it I might be inclined to just curl up and let
the world roll along without my help.

When I fall asleep the misery continues in a seamless
narrative of loss, pain, and suffering. It's a relief this time
when I wake up; reality I can deal with. It's the ghosts that
invade my sleep that bother me the most.

*   *   *

I tell Siri to turn off the alarm and I stand up in the dark,
wobbling woozily to my feet, then stumble over to the light
switch and let the real world crash on down over me.
My phone says it's 8pm. I need to get moving.

I check the drill: it's fully charged. I unplug it from the
wall and throw it back into the shopping bag along with
the other items I bought earlier, then head outside to start
the drive back home.

When I get back to town I detour over to the Piggly
Wiggly, and discreetly grab one of their mini shopping carts
from their parking lot and toss it into the back of the SUV.
Then a brief stop at my apartment is all I need to pick up a
spare set of my car keys, and I look to see if Jenny's been by,
but nothing looks disturbed. She must have taken my
instructions seriously when I told her to stay away from
this place.

The time has finally come, and I drive directly over to the *Early Riser*, keeping to the back streets and approaching the café from behind.

I park about a block away from the café then unload the shopping cart and fill it with the jugs of chemicals and toss in my little bag of supplies, then quietly push the cart down the dark deserted street.

I creep up as stealthily as I can in the still Texas night, but I needn't have bothered trying to be quiet. Security is the last thing the trio of men inside the *Early Riser* have on their minds.

Their conversation spills out through the walls and windows of the little café in incoherent jumbles of syllables and muffled phrases. The occasional loud profanity or burst of laughter punctuates the exchanges but most of it is just a tangle of sound. The occasional resonance of a heavy impact inside the restaurant suggests the crew is still hard at work dissecting the building in a desperate search for the location of Renault's mythical hidden treasure.

I leave the shopping cart tucked away in the shadows at the edge of the lot and pull out my little bag of supplies. The black SUV with the parking garage decal is parked behind the café in the same place as the last time I saw it. Tiptoeing up behind it, I bend down and pull out the potato and proceed to wedge it as firmly as I can into the tailpipe.

My former car is parked in the tiny dirt lot a few yards away from the SUV, thankfully just to the left of a splash of light that bleeds out from a nearby streetlight. I slip up behind it, drop to the ground and roll onto my back, pulling myself across the gravel until I'm staring up at the spot I'm looking for. The bit of reflected light from the streetlight is just enough to allow me to see what I am doing without needing to use a flashlight. I reach into my bag, pull out the drill, and start boring a hole into the underbelly of the vehicle.

I had been afraid that the grinding of the drill's motor and the screeching of the drill bit as it ate into the metal of the car would be too noisy to go unnoticed, but my fears turn out to be unfounded. The sounds are swallowed up by the empty Texas night air, whisked away on the wind like the noise from a distant air conditioner unit.

It doesn't take long before the drill bit punches through and I reverse it and draw it back out. I pull out the towel from my bag and tear off a long strip, then wind a couple of loops around the exhaust pipe and knot the end tight. The other end I push into the hole I just drilled, using the drill bit to stuff the material up into the hole. I return the drill to my bag and pull out the small bottle of isopropyl alcohol.

After loosening the cap just enough to break the seal, I upend the bottle above the tailpipe, letting a thin stream of alcohol dribble onto the fabric. Just for good measure I squirt a few drops along the length of fabric hanging down from the hole in the undercarriage, and when it's good and soaked I scoot back out from under the car.

Using my spare key, I pop the trunk open and reach far up into the dark space, padding around with my hand searching for the strip of fabric poking up through the hole. After what seems like an eternity I lay my hand on it and gently pull it through until I feel resistance.

As quickly as I can in my aching state, I scurry over to the shopping cart and push it up to the open trunk. I spread out what's left of the towel deep in the trunk, then proceed to line up all the jugs of chemicals on it, hefting them one by one up from the shopping cart and into the trunk. I remove all their caps and stuff the strip of fabric down and into one of them, then loosely press the cap back down onto the jug to hold the fabric in place. Osmosis will keep the entire strip of fabric nicely soaked in alcohol until the entire jug is empty, which should be quite some time.

The jugs are all wedged pretty close together so they won't be falling over, but the jostling of the car will be enough to send little geysers spurting out of their spouts. Within a few blocks the towel and interior of the trunk will be quite nicely dampened with a nice mixture of deadly flammable liquids.

Since the trunk release button inside the car doesn't work, after I close the trunk lid I break the key off in the lock. The trunk is fairly airtight, and combined with the cool night air, will keep most of the odour and vapours from the chemicals from escaping.

Grabbing the shopping cart, I back away as silently as I can, and then rapidly push it into the alley behind the next row of buildings.

If I were an intelligent man I would now hustle as far away from this place as my legs can carry me, but I'm too interested in seeing first-hand how this is going to play out. Thankfully, I don't have to wait too long. It's not more than about another half-hour before the back door of the restaurant bursts open and the trio of killers spills out. There's a little chirp as the SUV unlocks, and the three men climb into the vehicle. I can just barely make out their faces faintly illuminated in the interior lights as Ice Pick cranks the ignition.

The vehicle starts right up, but before he can put it into gear it suddenly stalls. The scene repeats as Ice Pick restarts it, only to have it stall again. After the third time there's a definite pause, and the doors open as the three men climb back out.

"Forget about it, Leon," says Ice Pick. "Besides, what do you think the auto club can do for us? It's not out of gas and the tires aren't flat. Those idiots are useless."

"Well what do you suggest, then? There aren't exactly any taxi fleets standing by to carry us to the motel."

There's just the briefest of pauses before Ice Pick says, "The asshole's car. We can take it to the motel and drive it back tomorrow morning then follow the auto club while they tow this piece of shit to a proper garage in a real town. I don't care if they have to schlepp it all the way to Odessa."

"Who's got the keys?"

"We left them in the ignition," says Tommy. "Didn't think anyone was going to boost it."

"Haw! You got that right," says Leon. "Filthy thing stinks like shit, too. We'll have to drive with the windows down."

"I don't care, as long as it gets us back to our beds. I hate this fucking shithole town. I can't wait to get out of here."

They pile into my car and I'm amazed to see how much it sinks under their weight on its worn-out springs. It starts easily and Ice Pick revs the engine hard two or three times for no apparent reason. Maybe he thinks he's driving a sports car. I hope he stops doing that – I don't want the fireworks going up while they're still here in the parking lot. Eventually, however, he must feel the engine is ready and they back up and drive away from the café.

I start counting seconds in my mind. My car's exhaust system is on its last legs, and so clogged with deposits it heats up pretty badly. I've been meaning to have it looked at, but, oh well. Too late now. I figure it should be anywhere between 30 to 60 seconds before the tailpipe gets hot enough to ignite the alcohol-soaked strip of towel.

I've only gotten to "46" when the peaceful night is shattered by the sound of an explosion so loud it almost makes my ears ring all the way over here.

The face of the buildings I can see on Main Street are all glowing orange in the reflection of a massive fireball that lights up the street almost to the level of daylight.

Well.

I'll have to remember that one. I wasn't completely sure it would work. Kids, don't try this at home.

CRISPY CRITTERS

I **AM SITTING** on the stoop of some long-since defunct Main Street enterprise, sipping from a flask and watching a couple of deputies setting little orange cones on the ground around the smouldering husk of my deceased automobile, when three black sedans with tinted windows come rolling up to the scene.

I don't normally hang around rubbernecking at accident scenes and had intended merely to stroll by and casually assess the results of my science experiment, but my eye was caught by the sight of a license plate partway embedded into the wooden door jamb of a boarded-up street-level office. Some of the water the local fire brigade sprayed on the smouldering wreck collected in a little puddle beneath the stoop, making the license plate, bobbing gently in the wind with its outer end slightly bouncing up and down, look like a short, wide diving board over a mouse-sized swimming pool. I had to lean over to pluck it out of the wood and decided it was easier to sit my ass down in the shade and to rest a bit than to bother straightening back up.

And twenty minutes later I'm still here, sitting listening to the buzz of cicadas and the occasional hum of an assassin bug whizzing by, fanning myself gently with the license plate and replenishing my strength with sips from my pocket flask. Far off in the distance I can see the shimmering mirage of a squat black blob hovering microscopically over the ribbon of black asphalt that disappears into the distance. It seems to be sitting motionless, floating in a wobbly holding pattern almost touching the horizon, but gradually it grows bigger and bigger, until it stops being an optical illusion and becomes a group of real cars that drives into our town and stops in front of my perch.

The passenger door of the lead car pops open and who should slide out but my old buddy the Ector County D.A.

He steps out into the street, dark eyes just visible under the brim of a big black cowboy hat, squinting into the sun and the wind and the acrid smell of roasted flesh, when he finally looks over in my direction and notices me sitting there in the shade. His eyebrows raise almost imperceptibly and a wry grin takes shape on his lips. Without taking his eyes off me he reaches into his front breast pocket and pulls out a pair of dark glasses and slips them on.

"Well, well," he says, striding over to me while behind him a trio of crime scene photographers and lab techs warily approach the wreck. "Why is it every time I see you I think of bad pennies?"

"I dunno," I say, fanning myself with the bent license plate. "Why is it every time I see you I think of abandoned dreams and crushed aspira—"

"Choose your words carefully, now, my friend," he says, cutting me off midsentence. "Wouldn't want to go ruining a good relationship with an ill-chosen phrase, now would we?"

"Is that what we have? A 'good relationship'?"

"Good enough for me to hope that perhaps you might be able to shed some light on this little barbecue."

"Aren't you a little out of your jurisdiction, Counselor? Last I checked, Ector County ended at Odessa's city limits."

"We don't stand on ceremony here. Considering my newfound acquaintance with one of this township's residents, I decided for myself to come have a look and check out some of the local recent events."

"I take it you're not referring to the supposed alligator sighting over at the Sanderson pond."

"No, as fascinating as that sounds, I'm really more concerned with last night's big explody thing."

"Now isn't that typical of you Ivy League types – trying to intimidate us reg'lar folk with your technical jargon."

Before he can reply, I add, "On the bright side, Counselor, the good news is that the hard-working taxpayers of Ector County won't need to be spending any more money paying you good fellows to track down my stolen car."

He raises his eyebrows again, not so imperceptibly this time, and turns to look at the smoking pile of metal and rubber in the street. His technicians are standing back assessing the char-broiled remains of the three occupants from a distance while the photographers go to work immortalizing the scene from several different angles.

"Now why didn't I already know that would be your car," he says, pulling a handkerchief from his back pocket and mopping the sweat from his forehead.

"It's sad, when you think about it," I say. "How people never take care of the things they get for free. I'm starting to lose my faith in humanity."

"I lost mine a long time ago," he replies. "It's the uncanny coincidences like this one that did it for me.

"Might as well go for broke, though, since you're in such a talkative mood. By any chance would the fellas who put you in the hospital be the poor saps over there in that car?"

"If I'd been beaten up by three large bags of charcoal briquets, I could give you a positive ID, but I'm afraid the guys who took me dancing had pink skin and full heads of hair. The crispy critters in that wreck don't resemble them at all. Sorry."

"Yeah. I knew it was too much to ask, but I had to try. What the County's going to save on looking for your car, though, will be all used up figuring out what happened here. It could be a long investigation and I'd hate to distract you from your healing process – you're coming along so nicely."

"I'm touched by your concern, Carl. I always knew you had my best interests at heart. Despite your trying to confuse me with your technical jargon."

"Well, how's this for technical jargon: 'justifiable homicide', self-defense', maybe even 'stand your ground'? Would any of those phrases perhaps jog loose a bit of salient information that might help me to put a big bow on this case and save the taxpayers a lot of money in an investigation that I'm pretty certain will turn up precious few clues?"

"I'm sorry, Carl," I say, grimacing as I force myself to a standing position. I hand him the license plate and blink tightly to clear the stars from my eyes. "That's not the information I promised you, notwithstanding my passionate desire to save our overburdened taxpayers the expense of a fruitless investigation.

"But as long as you're in town, I *am* ready to share the juicy details of the matter I promised earlier. Come see me in my office down the block when you're done here and I'll fill you in. I promise I won't waste your time."

I hobble away from him in the direction of my office. He stays in place, motionless, still holding the license plate, and keeps his eyes on me until I disappear round the corner.

CRIME AND PUNISHMENT

HEN **J**ENNY **ARRIVES** at my place she's momentarily surprised to find me in my office, sitting in the dark, my desk lamp providing the only illumination, with a glass of Scotch in my hand.

"Hey, babe, what are you doing here? Why aren't you inside? And what in God's name happened to your face? Are you OK?"

"I'm fine. Cut myself shaving, that's all. And the air conditioning's on the fritz. It's nice and cool in here, though." Like an actor responding on cue, the unit in the front window chooses that moment to cough out a sharp series of clicks, gently sputtering for a moment before settling back down and resuming its quiet rattling hum.

"Bummer," says Jenny, and drops down into the chair on the other side of my desk.

The desk lamp spreads an anemic little circle of light across the surface of the desk; the glow has just barely enough strength to bounce back up, reducing us to pale little disembodied faces floating in the dark. Jenny looks at me in silence for a few seconds. I'm not anxious to begin this, and I can feel a pit in my stomach gnawing away at my insides, growling at the prospect. *Just let it go*, says a little voice in the back of my brain. *Why screw up a good thing?* I squeeze my eyes shut and pinch the bridge of my nose with my fingers. As though that will make the voice shut up. I'm starting to second-guess my decision, but then Jenny starts talking again and makes the decision for me.

"So I'm dying to know – you said on the phone that you've got something to tell me. Have you seen Renault? What have you figured out? Do you know where Renault stashed all his money?"

I wish she'd asked me something else. Anything else. Why couldn't she ask me if we could go away, somewhere far from this town and its damned heat and bugs and boarded-up storefronts. Why couldn't she talk about moving to California, or selling her farm and starting one in Montana or Kansas or Nebraska, or even maybe just getting the hell out of the States altogether, and seeing the world? Why did she have to bring up the money?

"I'm very sorry to have to tell you that Renault no longer resides among the living, Jenny. His past finally caught up with him. He died well, though, and I know the last few years of his life were the best he ever lived. We should all be so lucky."

Jenny's eyes are wide with horror, but not with surprise.

"But that's not what I wanted to talk to you about, hon," I say quietly. "It's something else. Something that's been bothering me."

Her eyes change, and I can see the difference even in the low light. They get wary, and her manner becomes guarded. She pulls back slightly into her chair and tries to put an innocent tone into her voice, but I can hear the suspicion and caution in her next question.

"What do you mean? What's been bothering you?"

"Nothing dramatic," I say, watching her carefully. "Just a bunch of little things. You know how it is, small stuff that doesn't add up, or if it does, it points to conclusions that aren't very nice and lead to bad places."

She lets me keep talking. I have her full attention and she's sitting tensed up, exactly like the first time I met her, sitting in these same chairs in this very spot, except then she looked innocent and scared. Now she looks like a fighter slowly backing into a corner, ready for combat.

"I suppose what really brought it to a head was the uncanny coincidence of those guys from Houston showing up just a few weeks after Renault told us his story. I've been wracking my brain trying to figure out what could have blown his cover. How he could have been spotted in this invisible little town in the middle of nowhere, about as far off the beaten path as you can get in this country."

"Maybe that's all it was," Jenny says quietly. "Just what you said – 'an uncanny coincidence'. People come from all over to eat at the *Early Riser*. Or maybe word got around about the fantastic French chef and his little diner, and someone came by to check it out."

"That's what I thought, too, and I suppose I would have kept on thinking that, except for what happened one day when I was looking something up on my computer. I wanted to go back to a site I'd been looking at a few days earlier but somehow all my internet browsing history had been wiped. Luckily, there's also a separate search history in the Google search box that shows the recent searches. What caught my eye when I opened it was a series of searches that had been done for 'Mafia hotel massacre', and 'French Mafia'. Then a search for one particular man's name, which happens to be the same name that Renault mentioned as a bigwig in the French organized crime scene.

"And three weeks after these searches, who should show up in our little town but a group of thugs working for that very same man.

"Now that's what I call an uncanny coincidence."

There's no response to my comment and Jenny looks even more withdrawn into her chair, but there's a little trace of panic starting to creep into those blue eyes of hers, and she's beginning to nibble at her lower lip.

"I suppose when you figured out Renault wasn't ever going to spill the beans about where he stashed his money you figured half a loaf is better than none, and you made yourself a deal with the devil. What was the finder's fee he offered you? Twenty percent? Thirty?"

"Fifty," she says quietly. "Fifty percent and all I had to do was point him in the right direction. He said Renault would talk the moment he knew he was discovered. I never dreamed he'd go to his grave with the secret. I never wanted him to get hurt."

"Just what did you think would happen to him? Did you think a vicious killer would track him down from across the ocean just to pat him on the back and say, 'Good one, old man. You sure got me.'"

"Look," says Jenny, and her voice startles me with the hard

edge it suddenly acquires. "Renault knew what he was getting into when he ripped off a French Mafia boss. This isn't a kids' game. He started it. I just played my own part. If he'd just come clean we might all have gotten out of this much richer and in one piece."

"Renault was never going to get out in one piece," I say. "But it wasn't until I realised what you'd done to Renault that the other pieces of the puzzle started to fit. Once I understood what kind of person you are everything came together in a rush."

I pause to take a swallow from my drink and Jenny sits motionless without saying anything. The silence is like a wall between us.

"It was the bruise. That was a nice touch, I'll give you that. There's nothing quite as effective as a woman in peril to inspire a man to set aside his reservations and leap into the breach. When you showed me the bruise on your arm that you said Willie had given you, suddenly I didn't care about the other details.

"But when I saw you wrapped in a towel after your shower two days later there was no bruise on your arm. I didn't twig to it immediately although I knew something about that picture wasn't right. I was so distracted by everything else you were dangling in front of me I forgot what was missing.

"I might have gone on forgetting, too, except we stopped at your house later that day so you could pick up a change of clothing and some toiletries, and while we were upstairs I found a bag and receipt in your bathroom wastebasket from a party store in Odessa. You didn't know before stopping in to see me that you wouldn't be coming back home after our little interview, so you'd tossed it away without bothering to hide it.

But when I found it I knew what you'd done, except by then I was so smitten I chalked it up to innocent showmanship on your part. You wouldn't be the first woman whose report of assault was met with skepticism, so you could be forgiven for wanting to add a bit of emphasis to your story. The purple bruise stage makeup was the perfect touch."

"And what makes you think now that isn't exactly what it was – a 'bit of emphasis', as you put it, to inspire you to help me? I needed your help. I couldn't risk you turning me down or insisting I go to the authorities."

"Absolutely you couldn't turn to the authorities – but not because you were scared of them or of Willie. Because you weren't Willie's victim, you were his partner.

"You told me that Marty wasn't stingy with his money but he actually was, wasn't he? After he let you pay for your mother's nursing home expenses, he gave you almost nothing to spend on yourself. You drive an old car, and even though your clothing is nice, it's cheap. You'd look good even in an old potato sack, but you still want to wear nice clothes. When I looked in your closet I saw only three pairs of shoes. That's not the lifestyle of a woman with oodles of spending money – that's the lifestyle of someone whose husband keeps her barefoot and pregnant – well, barefoot, anyways – and makes her beg for every dollar she spends.

"You knew Marty was socking it all away and you couldn't touch any of it, but you figured if he died you'd get access to all his bank accounts and investments. You needed help, though, so you turned to the one person with even fewer scruples than you – Willie.

"It wasn't until I heard the stories about how Marty's parents and brother died that the penny dropped. You knew

Marty was terrified of dying like them in a head-on collision.
I didn't know what to make of the huge mirror I found
leaning against a shed on Willie's property until I drove out
and saw for myself the place where Marty went off the road.

"It's right after the curve, when you'd be driving straight
again. Not likely you'd lose control there regardless what you
drove over. But Marty didn't lose control, did he? He drove
off the road on purpose, straight into that tree."

"Now why would he do that," she asks. But her voice
is tiny, insecure. She knows what answer is coming and
she has no way to deny it.

"I already told you. Because he didn't want to die in
a head-on collision like his parents and brother.

"You sent Marty out on that 'beer run'. I don't know what
you actually told him to go fetch for you, but it was enough
to get him out on the road just when you'd arranged for
Willie to be in place waiting for him. And he was probably
half-lit from an evening of drinking. When Marty completed
the turn and he was suddenly confronted with a pair of
headlights that appeared directly in front of him, seemingly
out of nowhere, he had no time to think. He knew only that
he needed to leave that road immediately or meet the family
curse.

"He didn't know he was seeing the reflection of his own
headlights bouncing back at him from the huge mirror that
Willie had set up in the road, perfectly angled to be invisible
until the moment Marty's truck had completed the turn.
And because Willie likes to collect roadkill, he had a dead
armadillo handy to toss under the crumpled wreck, making it
look like Nature had orchestrated Marty's last ride, and not
a treacherous, scheming wife."

The blood has completely drained from her face, imbuing her with the appearance of a ghostly apparition. There's no point in denying the story, and her expression shows that she knows it. But that doesn't mean she's giving up hope. I figure in a minute she'll turn on the waterworks, but she's ahead of schedule. Tears are already starting to stream down her face, and her lower lip is trembling.

"So what if I did arrange for Marty to die," she says in a tiny voice. "He was a cheap, abusive, conniving asshole who used his money to keep me a virtual prisoner in that lonely house. Willie and I were supposed to split the money 50-50, and I was going to use my half to beat it for good out of this dead-end dump. But that all fell to shit when we found out Marty had locked up all his money in a ten-year trust fund."

"But Willie didn't let up on you, did he?"

"No. He thought I had more money, couldn't believe that I wouldn't have stashed away a big chunk of it before we sent Marty on his trip to Hell. He started making noises about telling the Feds my house was bought with drug money, so they'd take it from me and seize the investments too and I'd be left with absolutely nothing. I couldn't pay him what he was demanding so I came to see you."

"And used me to get Willie out of the way without involving you."

"And he'd have to keep his mouth shut about us arranging Marty's accident, because I made sure he knew that Texas has the death penalty for conspiracy to commit murder. Willie knew if he blabbed about what we'd done he'd be going to the electric chair right alongside me."

"But darling, none of that matters now!" she exclaims, leaping up from her chair and coming round to my side of the desk where she sinks onto her knees beside me and grasps hold of my injured hand. "That's all behind us, and we don't need Marty's money, or Renault's, or anything but just each other! We can go away together, far from this ghost town. I can sell the farmhouse and we can settle down wherever you want. We can be together and forget all of this nasty story."

"You know, Jenny, part of me really wants to do that, and I suppose we could make our escape and settle down somewhere and be happy for a while, but you could never forget what I know about you, and I could never forget what you did to your last husband. I'd spend the rest of my life sleeping with one eye open and looking over my shoulder for your next boyfriend to bump me off, too, and it would eat away at us. It's over for us, baby. I don't know how much of what we had was real and how much was you pretending to be a helpless damsel in distress, but whatever it was is gone forever now, and we'll never have it again."

That's all she needs to hear to release my hand and stand up, turning away from me with a stony, set look in her eyes.

"If that's how you want it, fine. There are plenty of men who'll be delighted to hitch their wagon to mine. I don't need you, and you can't do anything about it. So what if I called the goons on Renault, and so what if Willie and I worked together to eliminate Marty? You'll never prove any of it, and Willie won't open his trap about anything either. He knows the score. And until he sings, it's just your word against mine."

"How about my word? Would that count?" says a voice behind Jenny, as the door to my apartment swings open.

The Ector County D.A. walks into the room, followed by his two detectives. He's putting that little notebook back into his inside breast pocket as he walks in, and one of the detectives is pulling a set of handcuffs off his belt.

Jenny spins around and stares at me, wide-eyed. Her hands twitch and clench, and I'm ready for her to leap on me and start pummeling me with her fists. But almost immediately the madness goes out of her eyes and she regains her composure. Turning to the D.A., she says, "This looks like entrapment to me."

"Thanks for sharing your legal opinion with me, Miss," says Carl, as his detective gently takes Jenny's wrist and snaps on a cuff. "Of course, I don't remember anyone enticing you to do anything. I guess we'll just have to let a judge decide." And he steps aside to let his detective lead Jenny out of my office and onto the landing, where the last sight I have of her is the shimmering carpet of blonde hair as it bobs its way down the stairs and disappears from my life forever.

*   *   *

Carl and I are left alone in my dark office, illuminated only by my lamp and the light spreading in from the two open doorways. He looks at me and sighs, then sinks into the chair in front of my desk.

"I have to say, I'm not sure I could have done what you did, if our positions were reversed. You don't see women like that every day. A lot of men would be happy for whatever time they could get with her."

I'm still sitting in my chair. A small part of me is afraid that if I stand up my whole world will disintegrate around me, revealing the emptiness of my life and the magnitude of what I've just thrown away. I push a glass across the desk and follow it with the bottle. Carl looks at it and makes like he's

~ 221 ~

going to give me the standard "not while I'm on duty" objection, but something inside his eyes softens and he lets out a long sigh, then says, "Sure. What the hell," and pours himself a stiff one. We sit there like that for the next five minutes, not saying anything, just rolling the liquor around in our mouths and contemplating the infinite injustice of an uncaring universe.

Eventually, it's Carl who breaks the silence.

"We drove out to where they found you in that ditch and we followed the drag marks in the dirt over to the well you told me about. There's two bodies in there, alright. We can't get them out until tomorrow, though."

"When you do you'll find one of them goes by the name of 'Mendoza', and I believe he has some kind of interest in this region's Meth trade."

"*Hector Mendoza?*" asks Carl, with a look of amazement. "We've been wanting to get something on him for years."

"Well, I'm afraid you've missed the boat, then. The only thing you'll be getting on him now is a rope to hoist him out of that well."

Carl takes another long swallow of his drink. I can see him recalculating this situation, now that it's gotten real.

"I suppose I should arrest you too. You're not exactly an innocent bystander in all of this. There's a lot of bodies to sort out. And I'm probably looking at a new turf war breaking out to replace the Meth dealers you've been putting in mothballs."

"And I suppose you could spend the rest of your life prosecuting shoplifters and small-time gangbangers instead of making a name for yourself as the DA who cleaned up West Texas," I reply. "I'm pretty sure multiple homicides and international criminal conspiracies don't make the headlines in Odessa every day. Of course, maybe you don't want to become known as a crime-fighting crusader. Not everyone yearns for the bright lights of Houston or Washington. Passing a quiet, uneventful life in Ector County is probably exactly what you had in mind when you went through law school."

He looks at me sideways, a wry smile twisting his lips. And then he barks out a short, mirthless laugh.

"Of course you'd see it that way. If you don't like it here why haven't you left already?"

"Actually, Counsellor, I was thinking exactly those thoughts myself. In fact, I think a vacation might be just what the doctor ordered. Maybe a really nice long one."

"What if I told you not to leave town?"

"You wouldn't do that. Adding me into the mix would only muddy the waters. You've got yourself a nice clean murder conspiracy and several dead mobsters, along with the local head of a major Mexican cartel. If you need to assign blame, it's no stretch of the imagination to assume the Mexicans are responsible for the dead wiseguys. Car bombs are right up their alley. As a bonus for you, the Meth trade in this county will probably take at least a couple of years to recover if you stay vigilant. Why spoil the story with my sorry-ass tale?"

"You don't think it would add spice to the whole affair?"

"Sometimes, Carl, spice can ruin a perfect recipe. No, I'm afraid this is where our friendship takes a breather. But if it's any consolation to you, I'll always remember you fondly."

He laughs and stands up from his chair, straightening his jacket and adjusting his tie. I finally stand up from my own chair and shake his hand. I think it's the first time we've ever done that.

"Happy trails, pardner," he says with a grin.

"Watch your back, Counselor," I say, and shut the office door behind him.

*   *   *

I don't want to drive in the dark, so I sleep one last time in my bed in my apartment. I try not to notice, but I can't help but smell Jenny on the pillows and the sheets. I would have thought it would give me bad dreams, but I wake up at 4am feeling refreshed. Nothing bad ever happened to me in this room.

It doesn't take me long to pack. There's not much here that I want to bring with me, just a few changes of clothing and a book of true crime stories I culled from the lawyer's bookshelf in my office. I look sadly one last time at the little apartment before turning around and flipping the light switch. I was happy here, for about five minutes, and I want to leave before that memory fades away.

epilogue

'M ON MY way to the *Early Riser Café* on my final morning journey, but this time by car, not on foot.

I'm moving faster than I did on the mornings when I walked this route, but not so fast that I don't catch sight of the beach poster in the window of the travel agency. The chaise longue is still sitting there, empty. The little bikini-clad blonde with the Piña Colada never showed up, and I'm wondering if I'll beat her to it. *Time and tide,* the expression goes. The same can probably be said for empty beach chairs.

I pull around behind the café and park beside the big black SUV that's still sitting there, then get out and reach into the electrical box for the other spare key. I unlock the kitchen door and silently move inside and close it behind me.

The kitchen is deathly silent, and the first rays of sunrise are bleeding through the newspaper-covered windows, bathing the entire restaurant in soft golden light.

I walk into the dining room and survey the carnage. The walls are demolished, all the banquettes are torn to pieces, the lunch counter has been pulled over and the flooring ripped up to expose the concrete slab beneath. Blood stains still show on the parts of the café that haven't been completely turned inside out. Empty beer bottles and discarded wrappers from service station takeout sandwiches litter the floor.

I move over to the stack of paintings haphazardly piled in the corner. I pick one up and examine it in the light, then lift it up and bring it down hard onto my raised knee, breaking the bottom of the frame in half. Gently, I pull apart the two halves of the frame and carefully pull the canvas free. The top layer of canvas easily pulls up and I toss it to the side. The canvas that was beneath it looks perfectly unharmed.

I squint at the canvas in the light, and spot the signature "Aillaud" in the bottom right corner. I pull out my phone and snap a picture of it, then do a quick Google image search. According to artbuyerresource.com, the canvas I'm holding was sold five years ago by a private dealer in Paris for 52,000 euros. The buyer is anonymous.

I delete the image from my phone and from the Cloud, then loosely roll up the canvas and place it carefully on the

diner counter. Then I move over to the other paintings in
the stack and repeat the process with each of them. When
I'm done I have eight canvas rolls sitting on the counter.
I don't need to do any more web searches.

The broken frames laying askew amid the painted canvases
that Renault bought from the art school sit piled in the
corner, with no sign that anything has been removed. I gather
up the eight rolled canvases into my arms and quickly walk
into the kitchen and out the back door, where I place the
precious artworks as carefully as I can into the back of my
new SUV.

I'm about to drive away when a thought occurs to me,
and I go back to the kitchen and open the big walk-in freezer
door. A wall of frigid air envelops me and I sigh pleasantly
and inhale as deeply as my fractured ribs will allow, then
I walk into the freezer and look around. At the back, high on
a shelf behind a case of jumbo shrimp, is a black duffel bag.

I carry the bag out to the SUV and toss it in beside the
rolled-up canvases.

As I head east on my way to I-285 and New Mexico,
I catch a glimpse in the rear-view mirror of my town shining
ethereally in the desert, an innocent, pristine gem reflecting
the clean new rays of the dawn light. I feel a momentary pang
of great longing, as the little community gleams angelic and
unspoiled in the crisp clear air. And then a sharp *thwack!*
from the windshield jolts me back to reality, and I turn on
the wipers to clean the assassin bug's corpse off the glass
before turning north up the highway.

Did you enjoy this book?

If you did, then I'm delighted!

And if you'd like to see more like it, there's one simple little thing you can do for me that's worth its weight in gold (metaphorically-speaking):

Please leave a review!

Your online review will do more for me than you can imagine, and ultimately it will enable me to continue writing more books.

Plus, because I read every review, your review will help me to understand what you liked about my book, so that I can create others that you might enjoy even more!

THANK YOU, in advance.

--J.M. Holmes

About the author

J. M. Holmes was born and raised in Canada and educated in the Classics by Jesuits and nuns who would likely be disappointed to see the results of their efforts.

A Renaissance polymath, Holmes has been the Editor of the bilingual magazine for Glendon College in Toronto; the Editor of that city's French-language newspaper, *Le Metropolitain*; a successful magazine publisher; and Director of the Davis Film Festival in Davis, California.

Recipient of the 2005 *Heroes Award* from the American Red Cross, Holmes has also received commendations from the U.S. Senate, the U.S. House of Representatives, the California Legislature, and the City of Davis, California, in recognition of extraordinary charity work.

Holmes is also the winner of awards in California for running a business with outstanding environmental practices and from Rotary International for producing that charity's weekly publication.

Sadly, Holmes bears some measure of responsibility for the overpopulation of Planet Earth, having participated in the creation of two additional humans, Alex & Sarah, both of whom are college students working hard at honing their skills in questioning authority and challenging conventional wisdom.

Currently, J. M. Holmes resides in the United States and shares a home with seven feral cats. This is one of them:

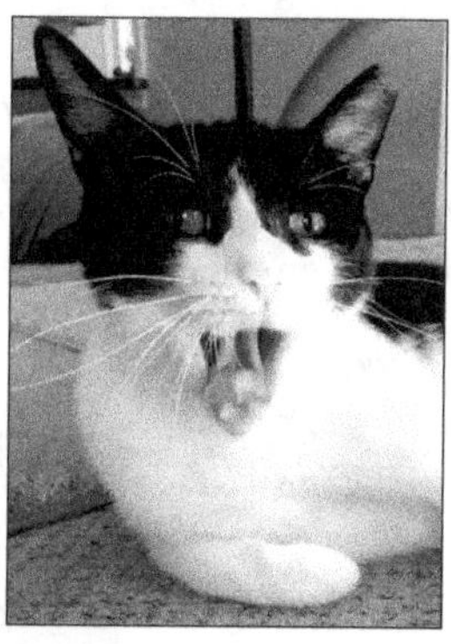

Be sure to grab this new anthology of scifi adventure stories featuring Holmes's popular duo, Jerry and Kat:

AVAILABLE NOW!

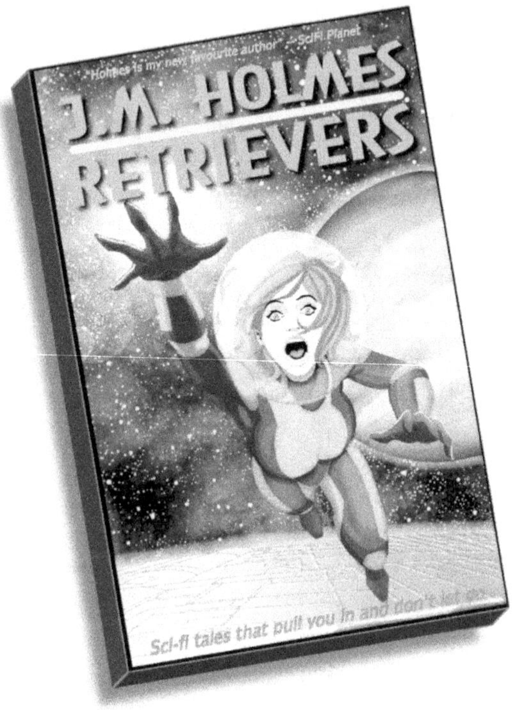

To be a Retriever means living a life constantly on edge, and when you're carrying a Discovery you're in danger every minute until you deliver your find to the authorities on Earth.

Kat is a Retriever, and she's one of the best. She's comfortable with her solitary life, trusting no one and depending only on herself.

It's a life that suits Kat well. That is, until she meets Jerry.

That's when Kat discovers that someone having your back can be a great thing.

Especially now that her competitors are trying to kill her.

CURSING SILENTLY, KAT scratched frantically for a finger-hold on the slick ceramic skin of the ship. But the surface was flawlessly smooth, without even so much as a seam or rivet point.

She was sliding faster now; she had no tools left to slow her velocity in the frictionless void of space. The hull passed by so quickly beneath her desperate grasp it was a blur.

To make matters worse, the farther she slid the more steeply the hull declined as the stern gently curved downwards. In a minute she wouldn't just be skidding over the smooth surface, she would actually leave it and drift off into space. She would already have floated off if it weren't for the ship's weak gravity that still gently pulled her.

But even now she could feel her every frantic scratch pushing her off just a little bit more.

The stern of the ship rushed toward her at breakneck speed. It was now a matter of mere seconds.

When the moment did come she almost couldn't tell. She was no longer in contact with the hull, and one second she was watching it zip by her plummeting form, and the next she had passed it and dropped off helplessly into the void.

She tilted her head back and saw the underbelly of the huge starship above her. As she slowly started to rotate end over end, she watched the ship move lower in her vision while her body did a slow-motion backflip in the darkness. Just as the last image of the ship disappeared behind her feet she heard the chime in her helmet as her suit announced, "All oxygen has been expended. System shutting down."

And her helmet – along with the rest of her suit – went dark.

Vedana could hear the keypad beeping quietly as someone entered the door access code sequence. A metallic *click!*, a pause, a hiss, and she heard a footstep inside the room.

She would have bet money that her breathing could be heard throughout the whole ship, it seemed so loud to her. She opened her mouth wide and tried to calm her racing heartbeat, which was humming along at around 200 beats per minute.

She heard the footsteps moving quietly about the room, but they weren't wandering around aimlessly. Whoever they belonged to knew where to go and what to do. There was a quiet efficiency at work here. She heard a few little clinks, a quiet hum of some unknown machine, and the ripple of a zipper being opened and then, a second later, closed.

And then… silence.

Vedana froze. Had she done something to give herself away or left some tiny sign of her presence here?

The intruder seemed to be standing stock still in the dark lab. Listening? Examining the room? What was he doing? Vedana wanted to scream, the tension was so extreme.

And then she heard a quiet footstep come closer to her.

Then another.

The footsteps stopped directly in front of Vedana's cabinet.

She gritted her teeth, and waited for the inevitable yanking open of the cabinet door.

Literati International

~ Since 1984 ~

Toronto • New York • London

Literati International is the privately-held parent company of Literati Media, established in 1984 in Toronto, Canada, which comprises Literati Worldwide Publications, Literati Broadcasting Enterprises, Literati International Reporting & Podcast Productions, and Literati Film and Television Post-Production Services.

Literati International has affiliate partnerships and representatives in numerous countries around the globe, including Australia, India, and Brazil.

Check out the full line of Literati-produced books and media at www.literatiinternational.com